MISADVENTURES

OF A

BACKUP BRIDE

BY
SHAYLA BLACK

MISADVENTURES OF A BACKUP BRIDE

BY
SHAYLA BLACK

WATERHOUSE PRESS

CHAPTER ONE

CARSON

"So I'm a little behind where I want to be in school, but the great news is that the DKEs chose me as their little sister in August! Isn't that awesome, since it's my last month of being single?"

I look across the dinner table at Kendra Shaw, my fiancée. Bubbly, flirty, twenty-two. Sweet, lovely, kind. She likes puppies and parties...but she has no idea what she wants to do with her life. We have zero in common. I would never have considered marrying her if I hadn't been coerced by her dad—my business rival willing to float me a loan so I can keep the confectionary empire I inherited from my late biological father afloat.

"DKE?" I ask, shoving salad around with my fork and trying to envision my life with this woman.

She tsks at me and rolls her eyes. "Delta Kappa Epsilon, silly." I must still look at her blankly, because she shakes her head at me, blond hair brushing her shoulders. "They're a fraternity on campus. The best."

Kendra seems proud of her accomplishment, and I try to be a supportive fiancé. "That's great. How did they choose you? Because you helped with the charity walk over spring break?"

"No. They pick their favorite Chi Omega each month, since we're their sister sorority. I may have influenced the vote a bit after I had too much tequila at the DKE end-of-year bash and danced topless. At least that's what my friends tell me I did. I don't remember." She winces. "Are you mad?"

Actually, I'm not. I should be. We've been engaged since April, and that probably happened in May. I'm just hearing about this regretful moment toward the end of summer. The man in me knows I should care that other guys have seen my bride-to-be's boobs. I wish I could say it mattered. I want it to.

It doesn't.

I keep trying to connect with this woman, figure out how we're going to relate to one another, and find some common ground. So far I've got nothing.

"Carson, did you hear me?"

"I did." I'm simply not sure what she wants me to say.

Deep down, I doubt she's ready to get married. Oh, she's enjoying picking out pretty things with her wedding planner. She's selected a grand wedding dress. I'm told it has a cathedral train that two of her ten bridesmaids will have to carry as she walks down the aisle. She's spent a nice chunk of her father's money to make this *the* event of the season. But I'm not sure she's comprehended yet that we have to get along afterward.

"And you're not mad?"

"Well, I don't think you should repeat that stunt."

"I won't." She nods solemnly. "I'm going to be a responsible wife soon."

She reaches across the table and grasps my hand, making promises with her blue eyes I don't think she has any chance of keeping.

I wish I could be enthusiastic. After all, I like Kendra. I'm simply not sure what I'm going to say to her for the next forty years. We're not married yet and we already run out of conversation in minutes.

"Are you really ready for marriage?" I ask her gently. "To be my wife?"

Her smile falters. "Is anyone ever really ready? I mean, we speak a few words, set up our house together, and try to get along. Isn't that what everyone does?"

No, it's not. I'm thirty, so I've seen a few of my buddies tie the matrimonial knot. Luis seems sublimely happy. Derek is really content and is excited for the birth of their son in a few weeks. Sam is already divorced and says he'll be an eternal bachelor from here on out. I don't know much about marriage except what my mom and stepdad taught me before they passed away. First and foremost, you should be friends with your spouse. You should like and respect the person you intend to spend your life with. Your significant other should make you laugh, be your greatest comfort, know you better than anyone.

My life would be much simpler if I felt that way about Kendra. I've tried. I've looked for common ground. We don't agree about politics or religion. We don't agree about where to live, how many children to have, or how to manage money. We might be able to overcome all that...if we loved each other. For months, I've done my best to foster a connection with her, but nothing has worked. And I doubt very much she's feeling it for me, either.

My head is telling me this engagement is a mistake. My ambition is trying not to hear it.

I shoot her a direct stare. "Don't you think marriage is more complicated than that?"

"Um..." She frowns, looking somewhere between concerned and lost. "I don't know. I guess we'll find out."

Her phone dings, and she lunges for it as if she's glad for the distraction. She flips through her messages with one hand and lifts her wineglass with the other.

A good five minutes pass in silence. She texts her sorority sisters about someone's botched home bikini wax, Instagrams her dinner, then waves at a passing waiter she apparently dated last winter.

She barely eats her meal and passes on dessert. I'm completely okay with that. I have her home by ten.

"Good night, Carson," she murmurs in her shadowy living room.

"Sleep well." I cup her shoulder—and hope the physical contact stops there.

With a wan smile, Kendra brushes a kiss across my cheek and escapes to her room. She moved out of the sorority house at the end of last semester and has been staying at her childhood home all summer. In less than a month, after the wedding, we're supposed to move in together.

I sigh. I'm past hoping sex will bring us closer. I know from experience it won't. The aftermath is more awkward than glowing. We haven't bothered in a month. I've been accused of having an overactive sex drive in the past. But since becoming engaged to Kendra, it seems completely dead.

That's not a good sign.

Suddenly, I see the orange-red flare of a cigar in the dark. The smoker inhales deeply. The pungent scent of tobacco fills the air. Gregory Shaw saunters into the room, wearing charcoal trousers and a pristine white dress shirt, despite the late hour. I know he's fifty-one, but he doesn't look a day over forty. He has nearly thirty years' experience in this industry, building his candy giant, Dulce Lama, from the ground up. By comparison, I've been running my late father's company, Sweet Darlin', for ten minutes.

Shaw exhales, leaving a cloud of smoke in his wake as he comes closer. "That didn't look like the satisfying end of a date."

It's on the tip of my tongue to ask if he thought I should have taken his daughter to bed, but he wouldn't appreciate the snark. This guy is brutally direct. I need to be the same.

"It wasn't. I have serious doubts this arrangement will work."

"Make it work, Frost. Otherwise, I'm not loaning you the twenty-five million."

Damn. He's got the bargaining chip I need. I don't see any way around that.

My late father's confectionary might be worth about a billion dollars, but I must have liquid cash to keep it from going under right now. Shaw has been salivating for the opportunity to get his hands on any part of Sweet Darlin'. He can't control me with the five percent interest I negotiated with him in exchange for some ready cash...but over the last few months I've come to realize that seizing power is his ultimate goal.

I wish I could sever the deal we struck in my moment of fiscal weakness. But that's impossible. Still, I can't let him think I'm totally out of options. "Then you're not getting any stake in my company."

He laughs as he cocks his head. "Let's cut to the chase. You don't want to relinquish any part of the organization, even temporarily. It bothers your considerable pride to be beholden to me—or anyone, I suspect. And you don't want to let down the old man, even if you barely knew him. I understand that. But what's the *real* problem, the one you're obviously having with Kendra? Isn't she a pretty girl?"

"She's beautiful." I can't give her appearance anything but accolades. When I first clapped eyes on her, I was patting myself on the back. Twenty-five million dollars *and* a trophy wife? Win-win. But as I've gotten to know her, I've discovered we have zero in common. I realize more each day that, as a couple, we're doomed.

"Isn't she kind?"

"Very much." I nod.

"Funny?"

Not in the way he means. She's comical when she's not intending to be, and not for reasons either she or her father would like.

How do I tell a man who potentially holds my future in his hands that his daughter is too immature for marriage? That I require a woman with more intellectual capabilities? That I'm too much of a serious-minded workaholic to make her anything but miserable? I can't simply blurt that our chemistry is nonexistent. I've tried that already, when I first began to have concerns. His answer was to send us to Aruba together for a week. It didn't help then. It will help even less now.

"Look... It's not that simple."

"Because...?" Brow raised, he draws furiously on his cigar with an impatient glance.

I rack my brain. Shaw will find the truth unacceptable,

somewhere between noncommittal and ridiculous. He'll deliver me another platitude wrapped in a threat—whatever he thinks is necessary to yank me back in line.

The simple fact is, I can't wish myself in love with Kendra. And vice versa. But he's more likely to hear what I'm saying if I assure him the fault doesn't lie with his daughter.

"Kendra is wonderful, sir. The problem is me."

He scowls. "Are you gay?"

I almost choke. Is he kidding? "No."

Most assuredly not.

"Then how are you the problem?" His voice is a razor-sharp warning to tread very carefully.

I realize my options are limited and I pick the best of an unpalatable bunch. I lie. "I'm, um...in love with someone else."

That takes him aback. The crafty bastard sends me a frown. He's suspicious, but he has good reason to be. "You told me when we began negotiating that you weren't dating anyone."

"I wasn't. I'm still not seeing anyone else." I haven't for months.

Climbing the corporate ladder back in LA after finishing my MBA a few years back, I was working seventy-hour weeks. Learning that I lost the biological father I'd met a handful of times was more of a blow than I expected. Finding out I'd inherited his empire stunned me even more. Some days, I still find myself reeling.

But Shaw doesn't need to know all that.

"I don't want to play a game of semantics with you, Frost. What the hell is going on?"

Shit. Why couldn't he just accept me at face value? Yeah, because he's too smart.

"Um..." Quickly, I try to remember the last woman I met who intrigued me. Her bright face pops into my head. Despite the three minutes we spoke, she left an indelible impression on me. "I met her at a party. Her date was the host. Because he's a friend, I saw her off and on before I moved here. Naturally, I couldn't poach. I've heard they've since broke up, but...in the time we spent together, I fell."

That's a huge embellishment, but the truth simply isn't an option.

Shaw stares at me like he's judging the veracity of my claim. "And you never saw fit to mention this earlier?"

"I'm sorry. I've been trying to forget her. Unfortunately, it's not working." I shake my head as if I have no control over my heart. "With all due respect, why not let Kendra find her own husband? She's a lovely, independent woman. I'm sure she'll meet someone—"

"She meets many someones," he drawls. "They're all deadbeats and louses. She has abysmal taste in men. My daughter can sniff out the worst loser in any crowd and be hopelessly attracted to him. So I made it clear to her that, if she wants her trust fund when she turns twenty-five, she'll marry who I tell her to."

That explains why, despite her obvious disinterest in me, Kendra hasn't bowed out.

"In five months, you've reversed a great deal of the damage done to your father's company during his protracted illness." Shaw sounds impressed. "It's obvious you're smart, resourceful, hardworking, and a leader. You'll take impeccable care of Kendra. And I'll erase your cash flow issue, which won't go away on its own. You have more loans coming due in forty-five days."

I do, and the bastard knows I lack the short-term liquidity to satisfy them. I have contracts that will pay off at the end of the year... but I will have defaulted by then. I've tried restructuring the debt, but it's a no-go. The interim CEO who ran Sweet Darlin' before my arrival panicked and used the entire company as collateral. If I can't untangle this problem, I'll lose the empire my biological father sacrificed everything—even me—to build.

"All that's true, but it doesn't change the reality. I can't make your daughter happy."

"Because you'll never love her?"

"Exactly. I can't give her the kind of devotion she'll want."

"She's too young to know what she wants." He waves his hand dismissively.

"Doesn't she deserve a husband who will love only her for the rest of her life?"

He frowns. "Not if he isn't in her best financial interest. You're far too smart to be this sentimental."

"I once thought so, too. But we all have a heart." I subtly remind Shaw that includes him, which is why he's trying to see Kendra settled. "Mine is taken. However, I still have something you want. You have something I need. There must be another arrangement we'll both find suitable and profitable."

Shaw falls silent for a long time, studying me as if dissecting me with a glare. I steady myself and meet his stare head on. If I can save this company without shackling myself for life, that would be the best of both worlds. Maybe I'll even stop waking up in a cold sweat.

"You know what, Frost? I think you're full of shit. You want free money. That's not the way the world works. There's always a price to be paid. What's this woman's name?"

I'm obviously a terrible liar because he hasn't bought a word I've said. I hide a wince and force myself to stay calm. "With all due respect, my personal life is private. Besides, you'll only hire a private investigator to look into her, and I've never told her how I felt. Something that important shouldn't come from anyone except me."

"Ah, unrequited love, is it? How convenient."

"I'm not finding it convenient in the least," I quip. "My life would be much easier if I could love Kendra."

At least I can say that with all honesty.

"Well, if that's not going to happen and matters of the heart are suddenly so important to you, I think you should bring this woman to North Carolina and tell her how you feel face to face. After all, unless you're able to win her over or find a way to fall out of love, you'll be alone for the rest of your life. So sad."

He's toying with me. He's trying to back me into a corner.

"That might be awkward. I'm sure she'll be shocked to suddenly hear about my devotion."

"Maybe so, but telling her also might bring great rewards." He raises a dark brow. "Remember, nothing ventured, nothing gained."

We could exchange parry-and-thrust platitudes all day. I'm over it. "What do you want?"

Shaw acts as if he's considering my question, but I know damn well he's already made up his mind. "I want to meet this woman you can't live without. If you win her over, we can talk about changing the terms of our arrangement. If not, and you don't marry Kendra, I won't give you a dime. I can't think of a single bank that will help you in your current financial position. And I'll be happy to stand on the sidelines and watch Sweet Darlin' crumble. Less competition for me. And maybe I can buy up the pieces on the cheap." He takes another long drag of his cigar. As he blows out the smoke, he snuffs the stogie. "You have a week to introduce me to the 'love of your life.' Until then, get the fuck out."

ELLA

"Hello. Ella Hope? I'd like to hire you to jilt me."

I couldn't possibly have heard that right. But the deep male voice on the other end of the phone didn't stutter. In fact, the buttery baritone gave me a shiver—until his meaning sank in. "Um... Could you repeat that?"

He laughs, breaking the tension. "Sorry. That was abrupt, wasn't it? How about if I start from the beginning?"

"That would be fantastic." I smile into the device.

"Hi, Ms. Hope. I'm Carson Frost. We met once—"

"At Shane's birthday bash in March."

"Right." He sounds surprised that I remember.

There's no way I could forget a man like him. If I had conjured up the perfect guy, the one who would forever make me long for sweaty nights and star in my masturbatory fantasies, it would be this one. He looks like a Viking someone shoved into a perfectly tailored suit. Blond, with sculpted cheekbones and a chiseled jaw worthy of Hollywood superstar status, penetrating blue eyes, and a mouth that made me wish like hell I wasn't there with his friend. His smile seemed somehow boyish and fatal at once. The night we met, just shaking his hand made me tingle.

"Mr. Frost—"

"Carson," he cuts in.

"Okay, Carson." How can I phrase this without giving away the fact that even thoughts of him screw with my respiratory system? "I doubt you have trouble finding women who want to date you. Why hire an actress?"

"Got an hour?"

I can't tell whether he's serious. He seems like the no-nonsense sort who's got a dry sense of humor, so I laugh. "Sure."

It's not as if talking to him is a hardship.

More like twenty minutes later, he finishes his tale. By then, my mouth is gaping open. To Carson's credit, he's really tried to make things work with his fiancée. I Googled her during his explanation. She's gorgeous, wealthy, educated... It says a lot about him that he's not hot to marry her simply because she's got money and looks. In fact, I commend him for refusing to make them both miserable. And he's tried being honest with her father about his feelings. The man simply isn't listening. Even if Carson is hiring me to assist him in a giant lie, I think he has some scruples.

In my dating experience, that's damn hard to find.

Not that my opinion matters. I need this job. I've got to pay my rent. Waiting tables isn't covering the bills, and acting gigs are too few and far between to contribute significantly to my bank account.

"So, you want me to come to North Carolina immediately to meet Mr. Shaw and...what exactly?"

"Convince him we're in love. I just admitted that to you today, by the way. You were stunned but thrilled. You think you might feel the same. We're going to try to cement our relationship over the next two and a half weeks, before my wedding. But at the end of that period, you'll sadly realize that your life is in LA, and I'm so busy with work that I just can't spare you the time you deserve, so you'll have to end things between us. Such a pity."

I'll give him credit for thinking his plan through. "Do you really think that will make your rival give up the idea of you marrying his daughter?"

"On its own? No." He sighs. "But Kendra will help me along. She goes back to school in a week, and there will be some frat boy who catches her attention. If I'm obviously uncommitted, she'll feel far freer to let nature take its course and couple up with someone who can give her a kegger and a good time. I suspect she hasn't told her father how she feels about us—in part, anyway—because she doesn't want to ruin my business. She's a nice kid, just one with oats to sow and growing up to do. Shaw is a businessman, but he's also a dad. He wants Kendra to be happy. I think he's hoping I'll settle her down, but she's not ready. He simply needs to see that."

"What if he does but refuses to give you the loan you need? Won't you lose your company?"

"At the end of the day, he wants a stake in Sweet Darlin'. I'll remind him he can't have that if the company goes under. Buying pieces from the financial salvage yard, so to speak, isn't the same. But with the right shove, I think I can save my company without marrying Kendra."

Carson Frost isn't just gorgeous. We didn't merely have the kind of chemistry that made my whole body zing enough to remember meeting him five months after a three-minute introduction. He's clever, too. And that puts him even higher on my dying-to-do list. Not that I'll ever actually do him, but a girl can dream...

"All right. I'll take the job." I definitely won't have to pretend I'm attracted to this man. In fact, this gig should be downright exciting. "For five thousand a week, plus expenses."

It's what my agent would ask for, if not more.

"Three thousand."

"I can be there in a day or two. I can be completely convincing as the infatuated new girlfriend. But if you need me that quickly, I'll have to ask for more."

"Ms. Hope—"

"Ella," I cut in. After all, I'm calling him Carson. And...yes, I want to hear the voice that makes me melt say my name.

"Ella, if you're able to drop your life to come here so quickly, how much work can you possibly be giving up as an actress?"

I wince. He's obviously used to negotiating. I usually let my agent do the bit where she shows her teeth...though there hasn't been much occasion for that in the last year, I admit.

I'm not a modern beauty. I've been told by casting directors I'd be better suited for historical films because I have a "timeless sensuality." In other words, I'm hopelessly fair. I have unremarkable brown hair and eyes, along with boobs and hips. No matter how much I hit the gym, there's nothing remotely waifish about me. But I'm a good actress, damn it.

Granted, pretending to dump Carson isn't exactly an Oscar-worthy role. Hell, I can't even add this gig to my résumé, but it will keep a roof over my head for another month or two.

"You have no idea what I have scheduled. I'm asking for this amount because it will mitigate my losses for abandoning other parts."

"You know, for an actress you're not a very good liar."

"Because I'm not in the habit of lying." I embrace roles. I get into characters' skins. I become someone else. I don't project an alternate reality of my own life.

I played a convincing Katherina in a regional production of *The Taming of the Shrew* last winter. I got rave reviews for my portrayal of Maggie in *Cat on a Hot Tin Roof* before that. My favorite role was Elizabeth Bennet in *Pride and Prejudice*. But more often, casting directors call me back for "other woman" roles. The last couple of months, I've been reduced to playing a princess at little girls' birthday parties. I turned down an "invitation" to become a stripper.

Something's got to give.

I can't give up negotiating. "Four thousand plus expenses."

"Thirty-five hundred with all the trimmings." I'm actually considering that offer when he drops his voice another octave to something that makes me shiver. "Plus a bonus of three grand if we succeed. I'll even throw in free candy for life. C'mon...help a guy out."

What are my more appealing options? My last dinner service at the café netted less than a hundred bucks in tips. I went to a couple of auditions that excited me last week...but no callbacks so far. I hate to leave my sisters for that long, but Eryn and Echo are grown. Well, mostly. Accepting is about survival. Still, I'd be lying if I said Carson Frost didn't motivate me at least a little. Out of everyone I met at that terrible party, he alone grabbed my attention and made me crave more. There was something about him...

"Thirty-seven fifty, plus expenses. And plan on paying me that extra three grand. We're going to convince Mr. Shaw that it's in his best interest not to force you to become his son-in-law."

"Done." Carson sounds pleased with himself. "I'll send you a non-disclosure agreement and a contract for your signature. I'll need them back quickly."

I probably should have insisted on more, but this is a good start. And if it takes longer than a couple of weeks to persuade his rival to back off, it's more money for me...not to mention more time with a blue-eyed Adonis who lights my fire.

"Of course. I need a plane ticket."

"I've just sent a message to my assistant to start working on that now. She'll call you shortly." He hesitates. "We should talk specifics, Ella. I have to kiss you."

Oh, when he talks to me in that voice...I can imagine his big body hovering over me, his head dipping, his full mouth enveloping mine. In fact, I can't wait.

"I mean, in order to make this work. We have to be convincing. I'll have to hold your hand, put my arms around you." He exhales heavily. "And kiss you."

"I don't think kissing will be a problem." I somehow manage to sound businesslike. For the most part. Though my girl parts are doing a dance, I have to be clear about boundaries. "But no more than that. I don't do nudity or adult work, if you understand me."

"No sex. I would never want you to do anything you're not comfortable with," he assures me. "But you have to stay at my place. I've got a spare room. I promise, you'll have privacy."

I pause. "I was thinking more like a hotel."

"No one is going to believe we're passionately, breathlessly in love if we're not spending our nights together."

He's got a point, but... "Won't it look as if you're cheating on your fiancée?"

"I talked to her earlier this morning and told her how deeply I care for you. She sounded relieved. It would be funny, if anything in this situation could be, but she encouraged me to 'explore my feelings for you, however I need to.'"

I bite my lip. In other words, she's praying he falls for me so hard that he calls the whole thing off. I don't have another argument.

"All right, then. I guess I'll see you soon."

"Good. We'll spend a few days getting to know each other, then I'll introduce you to Gregory Shaw. After that...we'll do our best to be convincing."

Hours of being near Carson Frost? Days of kissing him? Weeks of being "in love" with him, even if it's only for show? Yes, please. "Sounds like a plan. I hope we can make this work."

"Me, too. Otherwise, I'm out of options."

CHAPTER TWO

CARSON

My memory of Ella Hope didn't do her justice. As she hesitates at the threshold of my office, I stand, taking in her simple cream-colored blouse and houndstooth skirt. None of it does a damn thing to disguise the swells of those pillowy breasts or the grippable curves of her hips.

As I swallow back lust, I seem unable to find my brain. All the blood in my body has rushed south. The sex drive I'd feared had died since becoming engaged to Kendra roars back to life with raging insistence after one glance at Ella and her sloe-eyed sultriness.

Cora, my assistant, hovers nearby, watching me carefully. She's intensely loyal to this company. She might be old enough to be my grandmother, but she controls the flow of information in and out of my office with the skill of a PR master. With one act, I can set the right tone for Ella's stay. All I have to do is get closer to this woman, like I'm dying to.

"Hello, Ella." I speak the words like a caress as I walk around my desk. I can't strip her down and get deep inside her since that wasn't part of our agreement, but my tone says I'm waiting for that moment all the same.

"Hi, Carson." She sounds breathless.

Wondering how much of her seeming attraction to me is real, I smile and fuse my stare to hers. Pink rises on her glowing cheeks.

"It's good to see you." I take her arm, pull her close. She's soft. Shit, she smells like an olfactory aphrodisiac—lavender, vanilla, and something muskier I can't place.

I have to work hard not to bury my head in her neck and inhale her.

Ella blinks up at me as if our gazes are too tangled to look away. "You, too."

She's got the breathless girlfriend act down. Even I believe she can't wait another second for me to touch her.

"I've missed you," I murmur, dropping my head while delving into those dark eyes and long black lashes. And her mouth. Dear god, her lips are a perfect rosy cushion to take my kisses, cry my name, envelop my cock. I'd forgotten how fucking innocent yet sexual she looks.

I want to seduce her. Now. I ache to remove every stitch she's wearing and wrap my mouth around what I'll bet are glorious nipples before I kiss my way down her body. I'm sure her thighs would be soft and tender and beautiful as they're parting to reveal her succulent wetness between, which I would happily sink my mouth onto right now, regardless of the reason she's here and whatever else is going on in my life.

But I can't—at least not at the moment.

"I-I've missed you, too."

The whispered worship in her tone is perfect, and I doubt it goes unnoticed by Cora, who will spread the word when I ask her to. Right now, I'm too distracted by Ella to think.

I bend to the gorgeous brunette. Her eyes shut. Her lips part. I can't accept her unspoken invitation at the office, but if we have an audience at another time and in a more public place, I'll absolutely indulge in a long, slow possession of her mouth and enjoy every moment of it before I have to turn her loose.

For now, I settle for brushing a kiss over Ella's downy cheek, then look up at Cora. "Thanks for picking Ms. Hope up at the airport."

"Of course, Mr. Frost." My assistant gives me a crafty smile. Though she's never said a word, I know she hates the idea of me marrying the competition. She's never seemed impressed with Kendra, either. "You couldn't miss the meeting with your production team."

She's right. I'm still trying to win over all the workers—management and assembly line employees alike. The face time with them is invaluable.

"Lovely to meet you, dear," Cora says.

Ella smiles in return, still looking intriguingly dazed. "You, too. Thanks for the lift."

Then my assistant shuts the double doors of my office. Her heels clack across the hardwood floors until she settles at her desk ten feet around the corner. Finally, I'm completely alone with the first woman to trip my libido in what feels like forever. I have to back away or I'm going to do something totally inappropriate that will fall well outside the realm of our agreement.

I slide behind my massive desk again to put distance between us. "Good flight?"

"Uneventful, so that's the best kind."

Ella seems more collected now. Has she dropped the act or simply regained her composure now that we're not mere inches apart? An intriguing question to explore later...

"Good. I just need ten more minutes, then I'll be ready to leave. Hungry?"

She looks away, her stare landing anywhere but on me. "No, but I'd like to hit the gym tonight. Is there somewhere nearby I can work out? I'll do that while you're eating, and then we'll—"

"I didn't bring you here to starve you, Ella. I doubt they fed you on the plane."

"I had a protein bar. I'm fine."

Frowning, I stare. What's running through her pretty head? "Then you're probably ready for real food."

"You didn't negotiate meals with me. Unless we have a command performance, I should be free to fuel my body as I see fit."

There's a wealth of meaning in what she said. I'm trying to figure it out as I stare, study, dissect. Then I realize... She's an actress and she's not a size double zero. Thank god. If anything, I want her more lush, not less so. Since I'm a big man, petite waifs I could break with one good thrust do nothing for me.

"We need every moment to get to know one another. We'll be attending a charity benefit on Friday night. Gregory and Kendra Shaw will both be there. We have to be well acquainted and very comfortable with each other by then."

Ella crosses her legs, and her pose shows off the swell of her calf, the soft curve of her knee.

Am I really waxing poetic about her damn knee?

"We'll have all the time necessary after you finish eating. It's not as if we can talk much while we actually chow down." She raises a brow at me. "Unless you're telling me you chew with your mouth open?"

"Let me rephrase this. I've bought all your time for the next two and a half weeks. You're coming with me."

"I want a salad."

That's not dinner. It's a snack for a rabbit. "No."

Ella gives me a delicate grit of her teeth. "Nothing in your contract stated that I had to eat anything other than what I choose."

She's not budging, and this argument is wasting time. "A hundred bucks if you sit down with me and eat the dinner I order for you."

"If you keep it under five hundred calories and low on carbs, that's acceptable."

My voice drops, and I lean across the desk. I'm sure she believes her job is dependent on her weight. I get it. But the idea of her starving for someone else's shallow notion of beauty pisses me off. "If I'm paying you to have dinner with me, you'll eat a decent meal."

Her eyes narrow. "You're being argumentative."

"I'm being strategic. Some of Shaw's friends should be at the restaurant I've chosen. They'll tell their pal everything they see. You can't look like an actress."

She sits back in her chair and stares at me, plush mouth pursed. "Not every woman who watches her weight works in Hollywood. One fifty. Or you can let me choose my own meal, and I'll accompany you for free."

This may be a waste of money, but I'm not even remotely

tempted to agree. "One twenty-five and you have a deal."

"Fine."

I can't deny I enjoy getting my way. "Excellent."

I shove a few things into my briefcase. I'll have to work tonight to make up for leaving the office a bit early, but this time with Ella is critical. Nothing else I do for Sweet Darlin' matters without it.

She looks away and fidgets. I don't know what's making her jumpy, the job...or me. In either event, I can't let her visible nervousness continue.

Falling in love—even pretending to—virtually overnight won't be easy.

After I shut down my laptop and zip up my briefcase, I cross the room and hold out a hand to Ella. She swallows and slides her slender fingers onto mine. As she rises, she releases my grip and stands beside me. I'm struck by how small she is—even in heels.

"How tall are you?"

"I'm on the petite side, but I always wear shoes that maximize my vertical appearance."

Clearly, she's heard pushback about her height before. Tinseltown values women who are tall, beyond thin, and look as if they could fall prey to a stiff wind. "That's not what I asked."

She raises her chin defensively. "Five-three and proud."

I repress a smile. She is a tiny thing. Of course, since I'm six-four, most women I date seem small by comparison. And this one I'm pretty sure I could pick up in one arm and still finish a 10K.

"I'm not finding fault with you, Ella. Just asking a question. Since I'm supposed to know enough about you to be in love with you, I'll ask a lot of them until I'm confident we can pass muster in public.

I expect you to do the same. People will test us, Shaw especially. We have to make sure he can't trip us up."

Ella relaxes. "You're right. Sorry. Defending my height is a reflex."

"You hear about it when you audition?"

She nods glumly. "A lot. Nicole Kidman is five-eleven."

I grab my phone from my pocket and do a little Googling. "Eva Longoria is five-two. Victoria Beckham is five-four."

A smile creeps across Ella's mouth. "Thanks. I'll bet you can be charming when you need to be."

Once, I probably was...when I lived in LA and my most pressing problem was finding a pretty girl to seduce on a Saturday night so I could let off a little steam after a long workweek. Since Edward Frost's death and learning he named me heir of his enormous candy conglomeration, I've been sucked into a totally different life. For months, sex has been on the back burner. Hell, after grueling days and weekends of trying to wrap my arms around this business, I've barely had the energy for masturbation, much less getting laid.

Until Ella Hope walked through my door.

"I try." I escort her out the door and lock my office behind me.

Cora is already gone. In fact, the halls seem largely empty as we head for the parking lot.

"I did some research before I came. I hope you don't mind. I thought I'd get a head start on learning you." She looks up at me to gauge my expression, so I nod. "I'm sorry about your father's recent passing."

"Biological father," I correct. "He and my mother had a college romance and married briefly when she discovered she was pregnant.

It didn't last until my first birthday. Edward resented having to drop out of school to support us. My mother knew he had big dreams and didn't want to stand in his way. But it all ended for the best. Edward began experimenting with candy making and perfected his recipes while his grandmother was still alive to help. In fact, Sweet Darlin' is named for her."

"And your mother remarried a couple of years later."

I nod. "Craig was ten years her senior and came from a wealthy family, so that made her decision easier. But they were very much in love until they died in a car accident five years ago."

She frowns softly. "I read that. I'm sorry. Were you close to your mom and stepfather?"

"Very. Craig was my father figure growing up. Edward was always busy and lived on the opposite coast. He had priorities other than parenting." I pause. "I was a little shocked when he left the company to me."

"Did he have other children?"

"No." I hit a button on my key fob and open the door to my black BMW for her. "And he never remarried. After Sweet Darlin' took off unexpectedly just before his thirtieth birthday, he was committed to work for life."

Once she slides into the car, I shut her inside and walk around. Ella already has more questions by the time I ease into the driver's seat. "Why didn't he leave it to his younger sister, Sherry? Everything I read on the internet said she declined to get involved—"

"Totally." I start the car with a shrug. "She lives in Northern California in what can only be described as a hippie commune. Her son, Jagger, tried to take over between Edward's accident and the time he actually passed away. He made a mess of it, which is why I find myself compelled to hire someone to pretend to break my heart."

"That must be frustrating," she muses as I back out of my space and leave the lot. "Have you thought of selling the company? Then it wouldn't be your headache anymore. It sounds as if Gregory Shaw would buy it."

I tense beside her. "I won't let the company Edward devoted his life to building slip through my fingers. It seems like a poor way to honor his memory. Besides, it's the kind of challenge I've been wanting. There's no other organization that would hire me as CEO with my current experience. It's been a rough learning curve, but I'm starting to see light at the end of the tunnel. It's an exhilarating adventure."

"That makes sense." She stares out the windshield as the scenery zips past. "So...we need to know about each other, I guess."

"Yeah. How long did you date Shane?" I grimace. "At least I assume you're not dating him anymore. Or anyone else?"

Strictly speaking, it's not the first question I need to be asking. I should know shit like her middle name and where she went to high school, what she wanted to be when she grew up, her favorite color and food. But I find myself compelled to know if she's truly single.

She laughs, her dark curls sliding over her delicate shoulder. "Actually, I was with Shane that night on a blind date. When he saw the way you looked at me, he gripped my hand really tight...but nothing else happened between us. And I never saw him again. No chemistry."

The irresponsible parts of my brain are doing the samba. It's a relief that I can stop wondering if Shane ever convinced her to get horizontal with him.

If I had known they hadn't been dating—if Shane had mentioned that even once—I would have tracked Ella down. Well, I would have wanted to. But two weeks after his bash, I was called back to North Carolina to attend Edward's funeral and assume the reins of Sweet Darlin', so my life utterly changed.

But Ella is here now. With me. I want the lay of her romantic land. I know it shouldn't matter to me. But I won't lie to myself. It does.

"You didn't seem like his type," I remark.

She frowns. "Why? He's an astrophysicist. Am I not smart enough?"

"That's not it." I smile. "Quite the opposite. You're not bimbo enough. He likes them compliant and, um...dim."

She doesn't respond for a long moment. Does she somehow think I've insulted her? I can't imagine the insinuation that she's smart would upset her. But who knows how the female mind works? I jerk my stare from the road and glance over to her.

Rather than scowling, I find her laughing behind her hand, mirth sparkling in her dark eyes. "Seriously?"

"Oh, yeah." I nod. "Shane is a buddy. Really smart, obviously. But a complete asshole when it comes to dating."

That makes her laugh out loud. "I understand now why, despite his good looks and intelligence, he's single. My friend works with Shane, and when she found out he was dateless for his own birthday party, she insisted I would be perfect for him. I went skeptically but determined to be nice. It was his thirtieth birthday, after all. My first impression was that Shane is easy on the eyes and well employed, but not someone I could see myself with."

"How did the evening end?"

"I told him I had an early morning audition." She winces. "It was a lie. And he seemed fine with it. I hadn't even pulled my car out of the driveway when I saw him come on to a blonde in a dress the size of a tube sock."

Her description makes me laugh outright. "That's Shane. He's the kind of friend who would give you the shirt off his back, but a real douche with women."

"Hence the reason I never saw him again."

So I can put to rest any thoughts of losing a pal over this beauty I'm lusting for. "Good to know. Do you have any food allergies I should be aware of?"

"Fat, carbs, and sugar." She's doing her best to sound stern.

"So a prime steak, a baked potato, and something decadent for dessert it is."

Her dark brows knit into a little frown. "Carson, I—"

"We agreed on this."

"No. You twisted my arm. You know, you're not always going to get your way."

I plan to often enough that I'm not going to sweat the times I don't. There are perks to being the boss.

"Of course not." I toss a smile her way.

"Liar. You think you are."

"I didn't say that."

"It's all over your face. You totally think you are." She cocks her head. "How long did your last relationship last?"

If Ella is suggesting that my ex and I didn't make it because I was stubborn... Well, I'm sure that didn't help, but that wasn't the cause of our breakup. "About four months. Alexis was driven. When she received a job offer in Stockholm, she jumped at the chance."

"Oh." Ella nods like that's totally understandable. "Then tell me about your longest relationship."

I think back and back...and back some more. "High school. I dated Laura from the middle of my sophomore year until we graduated."

"Then what happened?"

Frowning, I try to brush the thoughts aside. But they're pesky, like weeds. When I yank them out, they only come back. Also like weeds, I have no idea where they stem from. They simply appear, full-grown, as if they sprouted and bloomed in a blink. "She wanted a deeper commitment before we both went off to college. She seemed determined to get engaged, if not married. We were eighteen. Too young."

"Did you love her?"

"As much as I knew how to back then. But we had different futures in mind. Her parents were high school sweethearts still happily married. She believed her life should follow the same path. When I looked at her folks—neither went to college because her mom got pregnant with her older brother—working tough jobs, living paycheck to paycheck, always dreaming about the weekend so they could all spend time together... That wasn't what I wanted. Plus"—I shrug—"marrying early hadn't worked out for my mom and Edward. Mom struggled financially until she met my stepdad, and even then we weren't super rich. Edward was ambitious, and despite the fact he didn't raise me, I still had that fire in my blood to make something of my life. Laura didn't understand why I wouldn't settle for a mere job. *If* we had married and made it through college, we'd be long divorced by now."

"That's a difficult situation. Neither of you was wrong…"

"Just different." I nod. "Our relationship was great when it revolved around football games, junior proms, and our first time in the backseat of a buddy's SUV. But we weren't ready for the real world. Or at least I wasn't."

"What happened next?"

I drag in a deep breath. "She married the boy next door—literally. They had two kids together. Last time I saw her, she wasn't very happy."

In fact, I remember the night my phone rang late. It was maybe three years ago. Laura wanted to get together for old times' sake. She said she wanted to clear the air between us because she needed closure. I drove across the Valley and agreed to meet her for coffee near our old neighborhood. Two minutes into our reunion, she teared up and admitted that she was talking to an attorney about divorcing her husband. Apparently, she'd never gotten over me. With her marriage in shambles and my own life being devoid of a significant someone, I wondered if maybe I had never fallen in love because I was somehow hung up on Laura. So I kissed her—once. I had to know if something still simmered between us that I had simply overlooked. But I felt nothing. I never saw her again. I heard through the grapevine that she went through with her divorce.

"I'm sorry. And none of your other relationships have been serious?"

"No. I've been career building. I've dated a lot of women doing the same. Coupling up hasn't been a priority." When did this conversation become about me? We're supposed to be learning each other. "How about you?"

"No one really serious." She gives me a self-conscious smile. "Toward the end of my sophomore year, I gave my virginity to a really hot, popular senior, thinking that would show him how crazy I was for him. The experience was terrible, and the next day he went back to the girlfriend he'd broken up with the week before. Then I dated the class president of our rival high school as a senior. But he got accepted to Berkeley, and I was set to attend UCLA. They have a great dramatic arts program, as well as a killer film school. So we did the usual 'I'll see you during school breaks' thing. But it wasn't long before he had a girlfriend up north. I was too busy working to put myself through school, finding time for auditions, and keeping my grades up to do much more than casually date now and then. Since graduating a few years ago, it's been more of the same—with a good exercise regimen thrown in. Trying to pay off student loans and keep the roof over my head is a full-time job, so guys have taken a backseat. Besides, have you met some of the men in Hollywood? Famous or not, they're unreal."

I laugh. "I assume they're all about their looks?"

"Exactly. And I'm selective because I make it a policy never to date a guy who has better hair than I do." She winks as if she realizes the mood in the car has gotten heavy and wants to lighten things up.

"Are you insinuating my hair isn't as nice as yours?" I say in mock challenge.

"I'm congratulating you for not wearing a ton of product or

35

sporting a man bun."

"Then it's all good." I pull off the road and into the parking lot of the restaurant. "For the record, what made you finally decide you should settle down and that I might be the one?"

It's my sly way of asking her what, if anything, she likes about me. Sure, I could coach her on an appropriate reply. After all, I'm paying her to be my adoring new girlfriend. But, smart or not, I want to know what she thinks of me. It's possible she doesn't give a crap and has only taken this job for the money. But I'm hoping otherwise. For a reason I can barely fathom, I want her to want to be with me.

That thinking is dangerous. I have my whole life on the line. Technically, I can't afford to be worried about Ella's feelings. I can spare even less thought about my own.

"Well, you're devastatingly handsome. That's a bonus," she assures with a wry grin. "You're kind but definitely not a pushover. You're strong without being overpowering. You're supportive and funny. And I like that you have goals and want to make a difference. I'm the same, by the way. We...click. What was it about me for you? In case people ask..."

"Of course. Just in case." I hold my smile in. I get the vibe that she wants to know what I like about her, too. That has to be a good sign. "You're beautiful. And not in that plastic, spray-tanned, need-a-lot-of-makeup way. My first thought when we met was how much I wanted to kiss those lips. Incidentally, that's true." I stop the car in a parking spot and turn to find her flashing me a flirty smile. "You're beside me unfailingly but you're not clingy. You're assertive without being bitchy. You're generous and sweet and patient. And yeah, I like that we're both passionate about our jobs and our lives. Like you said, we click."

Ella must like my answer because she flashes me a pretty pair of dimples.

God, she really might be the prettiest woman I've ever real or fake dated, not simply in outward beauty. She's completely authentic.

"Well, since we're so freaking happy, we should head inside and celebrate."

After her quip, I exit the car and jog around to open her door. She swivels in her seat to face me. Her legs emerge first, smooth and bare and shapely. I swallow as I hold out my hand to help her up. When she lays her fingers over mine, there's a jolt again. My heart starts to chug. What is it about this woman that's doing it so thoroughly for me?

I'm still trying to answer that question as we make our way inside the steakhouse. I come here often, and they know me, so we bypass the others waiting and are seated in under five minutes.

"Hello. I am Shen. I'll be taking care of you tonight." He's familiar and takes our drink orders. I notice he's trying hard not to look at Ella, but her blouse has shifted to reveal a hint of cleavage so it's tough not to stare.

As she orders water with extra lemon and inquires about the chef cooking her food without butter or oil, I study her. She really is classic. The curves of her face are softly female. Her sloe- eyed stare is so emotive. For instance, she's merely talking to this man about her food, and yet I see her concern, a bit of discomfort, and more than a hint of determination. I love that she's an open book to those who take the time to read her.

I wonder what her expression would tell me if I could hold her under my body and gaze into her eyes while I sink deep inside her?

"And for you, sir?"

"Water, as well. And..." I scan the wine list, then order a nice bottle of Pinot Noir. "Do you like that, Ella?"

"I do."

Her tone is both polite and dismissive. She thinks she won't be drinking any.

Shen nods and makes to leave.

"You can take my wineglass," she tells him.

When he reaches for the stem, I shake my head. "Leave it."

I'm polite, but I make sure he can't fail to hear the command in my voice. Immediately, Shen straightens and turns away, evaporating into the dark recesses of the restaurant again.

Ella stiffens. "You were lying earlier. You expect to get your way. You're used to it."

"Very," I confirm.

"I'm not a doormat."

"Not at all. It's one of the things I like about you," I assure her.

She meets my gaze and frowns. "I don't understand you, Carson."

Yeah, I don't understand me that much right now, either. "Well, that's what the next few days are for. Still game?"

The air conditioning kicks on. The artificial breeze tugs at a few strands of her hair, sending a lock to skate across her mouth. Reflexively, I reach over and push the skeins aside. And since I'm there, I can't help but caress Ella's bottom lip. Fuck, I want to kiss her.

Out of the corner of my eye, I catch some of Gregory Shaw's

country club and corporate buddies entering the room through an arch on the far side. No one waves in my direction, though. They've already spotted me touching another woman. It won't take long for this news to get back to their pal.

"Yeah." Her voice is breathy. "I have a feeling you'll keep this interesting."

CHAPTER THREE

ELLA

"Our audience has arrived," Carson says as he cuts his eyes across the restaurant to a group of suits walking in, dripping in custom tailoring and privilege.

I smile a bit wider and nuzzle into his broad palm that's still cupping my cheek. I try not to think about the fact that his hand on me is igniting my libido. "Is this what you had in mind?"

My adoring gaze is only somewhat feigned. And when his thumb brushes my mouth again, the shiver isn't totally fake. This man is freaking H-O-T. How are we going to live like a loving couple under the same roof for more than two weeks without giving in to the blistering chemistry between us?

Does it matter if you do?

"Definitely. It would be better if I could kiss you right now," he growls as if he's impatient.

His voice does something to my self-control that isn't good. Too bad I can't slide onto the bench on his side of the booth and lay a lip lock on him without drawing too much attention in this posh place.

"How about when we finish our meal?" he suggests.

The way he's looking at me—like he's dying to take my clothes off and make me scream—has everything between my legs throbbing. If his desire is all an act, he's the one who ought to be auditioning to become a star. I'm thoroughly convinced he wants me. That's dangerous.

"They should still be here by then, so I'm counting on it," I murmur in a sultry voice.

Yes, I'm flirting back. Every time I look at him, my stomach tightens and flutters like I'm a teenager in the throes of my first crush. I manage to smile somehow, but I'm all too aware that my gaze is inviting him to do far more. We're basically eye fucking in public. And it's the most exciting thing I've done with a man in years.

The waiter approaches slowly. Shen knows he's interrupting something, but he has drinks in hand. A woman in a pressed white shirt and black pants is right behind him, carrying our bottle of wine.

"Here you are." The waiter sets water in front of us, then grabs the bottle from the woman. Deftly, he opens it and pours a swallow for Carson.

He swirls it in his glass, sniffs the aroma, then tosses the liquid back. I watch him swallow. He's got massive shoulders and a wide neck, and the bob of his Adam's apple is somehow an incredible turn-on. I squirm in my seat as he nods the waiter's way.

I'm barely aware of the quiet man pouring us each a glass. The vino I swore I wasn't going to drink because it has too many calories suddenly becomes my lifeline. I really have no idea how I'm going to make it through this meal without crawling across the table to taste his mouth if I don't have something to take the edge off.

I gulp down three big swallows in desperation.

Carson watches me with a sideways smile that's sexier than hell.

"Are you ready to order, Mr. Frost?" The waiter looks at Carson expectantly.

"We are."

Before he can say more, I cut in. As much as I'd love to, I can't afford to sacrifice the calorie count I've allotted for dinner to this man the way I did the wine. "Is it possible to have a chicken breast grilled without butter or oil, and a salad with Italian dressing on the si—"

"Let me order for you, Ella." He delivers the words like he's a consummate gentleman who's thinking only of me because I might strain my delicate vocal cords or stumble on this complicated menu. "She'll have the eleven-ounce fillet, medium rare, and a lettuce wedge. Blue cheese is fine."

"Actually, can you make that steak medium, and add a house salad? And I'd prefer Italian dressing. On the side, please." I feel compelled to win at least a small caloric victory. If I don't, I'll leave North Carolina ten pounds heavier, not lighter. My next audition is too important to slack off. Rent depends on it.

Carson sends me a displeased glare that says I'm playing with fire. I don't know why me eating rich food is so important to him. But I don't ask the waiter again to have my meal prepared without fat or oil. I'll simply try to maintain the rest of this job and be extra careful when I get back to LA.

Not that the man waiting on us is listening to me one whit. He knows exactly who's paying the check and tipping him, so he looks to Carson for confirmation. My "boyfriend" nods. "That's fine. I'll have the New York strip, rare, and a Caesar salad. We'll take potatoes au gratin and lobster macaroni and cheese for our sides. Oh, and an order of that magnificent bread pudding for dessert with the Frangelico sauce. Thank you."

My eyes nearly pop from my head. That sounds like a billion calories. I shouldn't even have one bite...but my mouth is already watering. Why is he tempting me?

As the exchange ends and Carson hands the menus over, I've got a precarious hold on my temper and my expression—and I only manage to compose myself because we have an audience. Somehow, I smile as the waiter reads our order back to us. After Carson's approving nod, Shen backs away.

"That was high-handed," I remark, forcing a pleasant expression.

"This is my show, sweetheart. My rules." He pins my hand down to the table and gives it a squeeze. "You don't need to lose weight, by the way."

"Your opinion isn't the only one that matters."

"While you're working for me, it is. I like every bit of you exactly the way you are. In fact, if it weren't for our agreement and this table, I would be more than happy to come over there and show you precisely how much you turn me on. And for the record, casting directors who don't agree with me are idiots. You're beautiful."

I sit back and blink. He really just said that. Sneaky bastard. It's damn hard to be mad at a man when he's dishing out compliments. I could maintain my irritation when I simply thought he wanted to exert his control and show me who's boss. But he figured out why I was insistent, not to mention self-conscious, and flat-out told me he wants me. I don't have a defense now.

But that doesn't mean I don't intend to get even. After all, if he's feeding me scrumptious morsels that I'm going to spend hours in the gym working off, I'm going to give him a little torment in return.

"Am I?" I slip out of my shoe and slide my foot up and down his calf, sending him a come-hither stare that would do Marilyn Monroe proud.

With the wineglass halfway to his lips, he freezes. "Are you teasing me, Ella?"

I bat my lashes. "Why would I ever do a thing like that?"

"If you wanted a rise out of me"—he drags in a deep breath and glances down to his crotch—"you've got it."

That should not make me happy. I shouldn't care one bit whether his penis is saluting me. But I do. Why bother lying to myself? This man has big everything—feet, hands, jaw, chest. I'll bet he's big all over, and I have to repress a shiver just thinking about it.

Maybe I should stop toying with Carson, cease playing a dangerous game that can't lead anywhere except to bed. Can I really take our supposedly pretend flirtation to places I said I wouldn't go during our negotiation, then back away from the seemingly inevitable later?

Not really...but the responsible reply is not what comes out of my mouth.

"What if I don't believe you?" I ask him in a breathy voice, then lick my bottom lip for good measure.

Carson never takes his eyes off me. Oh, his gaze follows my tongue, then dips down to the shadowy opening of my shirt. But he merely continues to caress a thumb over the back of my hand and leans back slightly. "You don't want to take my word for it?"

I could but...suddenly, I know exactly how to make his torment so much worse. I slide my foot up his leg again, dragging my toe across his thigh. "No. I'm a girl who likes *hard* proof." My taunt has barely left my mouth when I settle my sole over something so steely and massive I do a double take and stare at him as if I can't comprehend what I feel. "Oh, my god. Seriously?"

He sends me another crooked smile as if he's mighty pleased that he could shock me. "Every inch of that is for you, and if you don't get your foot off of me now, I'm going to forget we have a bargain and that I'm a gentleman."

His words and hot stare grip my insides and squeeze until I'm breathless. What do I do? Carson strikes me as the sort of man who means every word he says. If I'm not careful, I'll find myself in over my head. After all, I'm sure he has far more experience than me.

That's all true...and yet I can't seem to resist teasing him.

"We're in public with a table between us." I wriggle my toes against his cock. "You can't stop me."

He sucks in a bracing breath, anchoring a fist on the gleaming wood. His knuckles turn white. "First, who says I want to stop you? Second, you should understand that if you continue, you're opening yourself to merciless retribution the moment we're alone."

Promise? "That wasn't in our agreement."

"Neither was this." He glances at my toes fluttering all over his cock.

I smile. "If it's bothering you that much, I can stop."

Carson unfolds his napkin, drops it over his lap, and seemingly smooths it with his hands. But beneath the cloth he grabs my ankle, which feels completely enveloped in his huge hands, and pulls me against his hard ridge. "If you move your foot an inch before I tell you to, I will torment the hell out of you before we leave this restaurant."

I'm tempted to test him, just to see what he'll really do. Of course it's not smart, but I'm enjoying this way too much to stop now. "Oh? How will you do that?"

"I have a theory." His hands tighten on my arch and heel before he slides my sole over his erection again, all but baring his teeth in pleasure at the friction. Then slowly, he skates his palm over the ball and up my toes before lifting his fingers away to wrap around his wineglass. He takes a gulp.

"What?"

"That little girls like you never think of all the underhanded ways a man like me can repay her for this kind of agony. But I could, quite simply. All I have to do is this."

He crooks a finger and drops it under the table to drag it softly and slowly up my foot from heel to toe. He lingers over the arch, agitating the nerves there with a barely there scrape. I jolt at the sensation, trying to jerk my foot away and doing my best not to gape because Shaw's friends are watching our every move.

"Carson, don't," I whisper. "I'm ticklish."

"Then I guessed right." And his smile looks smug.

"If you don't quit, I'm going to giggle." I'm already biting my lip to hold my startled laugh in. "We're being watched as we speak."

"You should have thought of that. Now you have to live with the consequences until dinner arrives. But that's not the only one."

Before I can protest, he changes tactics, gripping my foot and massaging it thoroughly—arch, ball, toes—up, then back down again until I'm melting. I like this better than his tickling. Way better.

My head falls back as my eyes close. It's all I can do not to groan.

"Oh, that's really good."

"And now every man in this room wants to know what I'm doing to put that look of pleasure on your face."

He's right, and I struggle to open my eyes and straighten out my expression, but he alternates by tickling and massaging my foot until I feel worked up and wrung out under his hands. I'm doing my best to fight back, pressing against his unflagging erection to disarm him. But he's toying with me, only letting me skate over his massive length when he allows it. The rest of the time, he's manipulating me—figuratively and literally.

I'm no match—at the moment.

"Give up?"

Maybe I should. But end this delicious game because I'm currently losing? "It's not over yet."

"I would have never guessed this, but I think you like living dangerously."

I never imagined that to be true. I'm rethinking myself now. He makes me wild. He makes me dare to let the woman inside me free.

"You think you have me all figured out? Did you know I'm stubborn, too?" Into his silence, I nod. "Incredibly. If I can't undo you with my toes"—I wiggle them for effect and work my way up to the head of his thick crest trying to poke out of his slacks, eliciting a low, gratifying groan—"then I'll do my best to take you apart with my words."

"Will you?"

I nod. "Want to know what I thought the first time I saw you? Kissing you, absolutely. But that's the least of what went through my head. I wanted to climb your body, taking my clothes off as I made my way up and wrapped my legs around you. I wanted to drag my tongue up the tendons of your neck and kiss my way across your chest as I stripped off your shirt to see if you're really as broad and muscled as you look. *Then* I wanted to tear off your pants and fall into your eyes as you thrust inside my body."

I let the words hang there for a long moment, gratified by his harsh, audible breathing.

"My second thought was that you might be more man than I'm able to handle...but I wanted to try."

"Do you still want to?"

I could be less than honest and end this verbal foreplay here, but why? "I'm desperate to."

Carson doesn't move for a long moment. Our waiter drops something off two tables away, then passes by. Suddenly, my boss/boyfriend snaps his fingers to get Shen's attention.

"Yes, sir?" He keeps his dark eyes fixed on Carson's face, but somehow I think he's aware of what's going on under the table. He's probably seen it all and I doubt he misses much.

"I'd like the check and our food to go. We need to be out of here in five minutes."

I repress a tremor. Oh, yeah. I'm getting to him.

The question is...what am I going to do about it?

If Carson's request is unusual, Shen doesn't show it. "Of course. I'll have the kitchen pack up everything for you right away."

The waiter disappears, and Carson tosses back the last of his wine, then pours us each more, finishing off the bottle. "If you're so inclined, drink fast. We're leaving ASAP."

"Already?"

He sends me a smile that could singe me alive. "You started this, so you're going to pay the consequence."

Oh, goody. "I'm not worried."

"That's your first mistake, Ella. But I'm glad to hear it. That will make the moans and screams of surrender I wring from you when we get to my place even sweeter."

I drag my foot across his crotch one more time just to make sure I have his attention. Yep. I do. No doubt. He's still as big and hard as ever. I'm baiting the sexy bear. I might regret this later. Right now, I don't care one whit.

Lifting my lips into a smile, I flirt his way. "We're supposed to be getting to know each other. Shouldn't we focus on that?"

"Oh, we will," he vows, pressing his thumbs into the tight arch of my foot before working his way up my calf. "By morning, I'm hoping we know each other really fucking well."

My heart kicks into high gear. My entire body tenses. None of this is logical or even helpful to the cause, but the devil on my shoulder—the one that insists this man is way too delicious to pass up for a two-week fling—says that always being the dutiful good girl is both boring and overrated. If Carson Frost wants to take me to bed, smart or not, I'm going to let him curl my toes and unravel my body.

"Here you are, sir." Shen hands Carson the check, then sets down several bags emblazoned with the steakhouse's name and logo.

Heat emanates from them, and the aromas make my mouth water. I can't even remember the last time I indulged in red meat and cheesy potatoes. Everything smells magnificent. But my aching pussy has an agenda all its own: letting Carson do his worst to me—

fast.

"Thanks." He slaps his napkin on the table, regretfully releases my foot, and reaches into his wallet to withdraw his credit card. "There's an extra ten percent for you if you're able to close my tab out in under two minutes."

Shen smiles. "Of course, sir."

"Excellent." Carson watches the waiter hustle away, then stands, buttoning his coat over his erection while giving a subtle glance to Gregory Shaw's watchful pals. "That gives me at least a minute to kiss the hell out of you. Stand up, Ella."

As I wedge my foot back into my shoe, my stomach knots into a tight ball. As uncomfortable as that is, it's got nothing on the ache throbbing between my legs as I wobble upright and rest my palm on the back of the booth so I can find balance. I drag in a steadying breath.

Carson doesn't bother with pretty words or preamble. He grabs me around the waist and aligns our bodies. He's so close, I feel the press of every rigid inch of him. I look my way up the long line of his muscled torso until our stares collide. His piercing blue eyes steal my breath. Maybe that sounds cheesy, but I have never met a man who can unwind all my thoughts and resistance so quickly and with so little effort.

He winds his free hand around my nape and positions my face under his—exactly where he wants it. As he swoops down toward me, the restaurant fades away. My ears hear only my own frantic heartbeat and his rough breaths. My blood sizzles. My thoughts race. I'm no longer aware of the air-conditioned breeze chilling my skin or the group of gossipy men watching us. I'm zeroed in on Carson Frost and feeling his mouth cover mine.

"Want to stop me?" he murmurs as his lips hover just over mine.

I don't think at all about my reply. "No."

"Then give me your mouth, Ella. Don't hold anything back. I'm not going to."

That's all the warning I get before he wraps his fingers in my hair and takes possession. He nudges my lips open and steals inside as if he has every right to be there. Then he thrusts in to sample my depths, mingle our breaths...and steal my soul.

I lift myself on tiptoes to allow him deeper access. I grab his lapels to steady myself. And I rub against him. His kiss is everything I suspected—demanding, powerful, arousing on a level I've never experienced. I'm dizzy. I'm delirious. I'm loving it.

I don't want to think about the future.

I know this is a job, and I shouldn't be so hot to go to bed with the man who's hired me. This is a line I never thought I would cross with any employer, for any role.

Carson—and the way he touches me—robs me of my ability to refuse him anything.

I moan into his mouth. He grabs my dress in his fist and tries futilely to pull me closer still. The thought that whatever happens with this man between the sheets is going to surpass everything I've ever felt and ruin me for any other man streaks across my brain. Even that doesn't stop me from tossing myself headlong into this staggering passion.

I want him now.

Nearby, a man clears his throat. Carson lifts his head and snaps around to the sound. I blink in the general direction of the intrusion, hazy and off-balance and deeply resentful that I no longer have his lips on mine.

Shen is standing there, leather billfold in hand. "I apologize for interrupting. You indicated time was of the essence."

"Absolutely. Thank you." Carson grabs his credit card, dashes the pen over the slip of paper, then shoves it back at Shen as he lifts both big bags with one sweep of his long fingers. He clutches my hand with the other and gives me a stare that assures me I'm about to experience pleasure like I've never imagined.

I yank him toward the door. "Let's go."

Carson sends me a sharp nod, and we're off. I spare one last glance for his rival's upper-crust friends. They're staring at us as they fiddle with their phones. "I think one of those suits may have snapped a picture of us kissing and sent it to Shaw."

"Great." He reaches around me and shoves the door open. His voice sounds as if he couldn't give a damn what his competitor's cronies might have done. He merely wants to be away from this restaurant and find someplace private so he can finish dismantling what's left of my defenses. He wants to conquer me. Heaven help me, I want to let him.

This is so not what I planned on happening when I boarded the plane at quarter before ten this morning in sunny Los Angeles. But this is so much better.

As we exit the restaurant, the evening humidity envelops me. Since I'm a West Coast girl, I'm not used to that. Traffic noise on the road nearby and the faint song of cicadas competes with the sound of Carson's rapid footsteps eating up the blacktop and the gong of my racing heart. When we reach the car, he unlocks it, slides the food into the backseat, then slams the door. Then he pins me against his sleek black vehicle. His wide palms cover the space around me. He sucks away all the available air between us simply by being.

"Carson…"

"Are you protesting now that we're alone?"

"No." I assure with a shake of my head. "I was going to tell you to hurry up."

"I intend to." He grimaces as if he's reluctant to admit what he's going to say next. "But I can't not taste your mouth right now."

I don't even have time to gasp before he seizes my lips again, forcing his way inside my mouth and sweeping every inch. His breath is harsh, his kiss reckless. But his touch skimming down my body is so gentle that I sigh into him and work my arms around his neck to pull him closer.

We kiss forever, it seems. Every time I think he's going to back off and drive us out of this parking lot, away from the cars honking at our PDA, he fuses our lips together again and delves even deeper than before. I don't merely melt against him this time, I become one with him, remolded to him by the heat of our bodies and our growing need.

Finally, he wrenches away with a curse, raking his hand through his hair. "If we don't leave now, I'll do something to you right here that we could get arrested for."

I wipe away the traces of my lipstick from his mouth as he opens my car door and ushers me into my seat. A moment later, he's tossing himself into the vehicle beside me, revving the engine, and peeling out onto the street. The aroma of dinner fills the car, but that's not the hunger twisting me up inside.

"How long until we reach your place?" I murmur, dropping a hand on his thigh.

For some reason, I can't bring myself to stop touching this man.

He grimaces. "Usually ten minutes. I'll try to make it in five."

The last of the rush-hour traffic seems to be clearing out, so I'm hopeful he can make that happen.

"Once we hit the door, everything you're wearing better evaporate quickly or I'll rip it off your body. Do you hear me, Ella? Unless you're saying no. If you intend to stop me, now's the time, sweetheart."

It's awesome that he keeps trying to give me an out. He wants full consent, and I respect that. I should probably take the exit he's repeatedly offered me. It would be smarter.

But when it comes to Carson Frost, I'm losing IQ points by the minute.

"I could say the same to you."

"What do you mean?" He sends me a sharp stare.

"When we get behind your closed door, those clothes better come off fast, mister."

Despite the arousal pouring off his big body, a faint smile creases his lips. "You're an unpredictable woman."

"Don't you forget it."

As he speeds toward his place, I'm looking for something to focus on besides how badly I want him. If I don't distract myself, I'll likely speak or act in some way to put a dent in his focus and compromise our safety.

Thankfully, Carson fills the void. "In case we don't come up for air again until we meet Shaw and his daughter on Friday night, my middle name is Alexander. I was born in Northridge. I graduated from Reseda High School, did my undergrad at UC Irvine, and got my MBA from USC. Give me your details."

I watch him steer the speeding car steadily and wonder how he's managing it. I don't think I can retain a word of what he said. I'm not even sure I can spit out my own personal information. All I can think about is how amazing it will feel when I have this man's naked body pressing into mine. Did he say we wouldn't come up for air for two days?

"Um... My middle name is Cooper. It's a family name. I-I was born in Simi Valley. I went to Simi Valley High. Go Pioneers..." The stupid joke slips off my tongue. "And I graduated from UCLA. How much longer before we can get naked?"

The car lurches forward as he steps on the gas a bit harder. "I'm trying to get there as fast as I can and still stay in one piece. Are you really ready for what's about to happen?"

If I don't have this man inside me soon, I'll freaking fall apart.

"Absolutely."

CHAPTER FOUR

CARSON

Dinner took a totally unexpected turn—and I love where this is heading. When I greeted her at the office earlier, I thought this would be the longest two and a half weeks of my life. I couldn't imagine being close to Ella every waking moment yet not succumbing to the urge to seduce her. At least not without losing my mind. Now, I'm pretty sure the second we cross the threshold of my pad and shut the door behind us, we're going to be naked, entwined, and busy.

Hallelujah!

It sounds odd, but from the moment I saw her again, I've felt as if my to-do list would never be complete if I didn't get the chance to do Ella Hope. Over the phone, I had the impression she was prim, maybe even a bit shy sexually. I could call the woman who felt up my hard cock with her wriggling toes under the table in a restaurant a lot of things, but I'm scratching shy off the list. God knows I can't look at her flushing cheeks, gleaming eyes, and the outline of her hard nipples through that silky blouse for much longer without stripping her down and tasting her all over.

She's gripping the armrest of her door, foot tapping the

floorboard, as I make the last few turns and lurch into the complex I've been renting an apartment at until I get Sweet Darlin' in order. Then I'll focus on putting down roots and buying a house.

For now, I careen into the nearest parking spot and throw the car into park. "We're here."

But she's already out the door. Ella seems almost as eager as I am. I love the fact that she coyly teased me through our abruptly shortened dinner. But now that the moment is here, she's not toying with me at all.

She slams her car door. I reach in and grab the food, then lock up the car behind me. "I'll get your suitcase later."

After I've had an hour or two inside her, I might be able to leave her for a few minutes without the craving for her hitting me so hard I can't function. Maybe.

"Much later." Ella gives me an impatient glance, silently asking me to lead the way.

I envelop her hand in mine and all but drag her toward the building on the right, then up a flight of stairs. At my front door, I shove the key into the lock and turn it. "Get ready. This is going to be fast."

"I hope so," she mutters, relief all over her face when the door gives way and admits us into the silent, shadowy apartment.

With a hand on the small of her back, I guide her inside and shut the door behind me, locking it. I pocket the keys and take a handful of ground-eating steps to the kitchen. I shove the bags of food in the refrigerator, then turn back to her as the door swings shut. I'm already tearing off my tie, stripping out of my shirt.

Ella stands at the threshold of my kitchen, watching, breathless.

"Come here, little girl."

She raises her chin. "I'm a grown woman."

"And I can't wait to feel every inch of you. I'm going to swallow you whole." I toss my tie on the floor, then yank my shirt off my shoulders, not bothering with the cuffs. The buttons ping off. Fuck them. I'll worry about that later.

"You can try." She saunters forward, kicking off her shoes and reaching behind her to undo the button of her skirt at the small of her back.

I hear the hiss of her zipper falling. My skin tightens. My heart revs. My cock screams.

Finally, Ella is within reach, so I grab her around the waist and lift her onto my kitchen island. She weighs next to nothing. I settle her in the middle, pressing one hand to her abdomen to lay her back while using the other to shove the houndstooth that falls to her knees up around her hips.

When I catch sight of her panties, I freeze. Stare. Blink. Forget to breathe.

To call her underwear a scrap of fabric would be generous. It's white and feminine. It taunts me with the fact it's almost sheer...but not quite. The lace at the front is shaped like a butterfly and it barely covers her pussy. Two strips of fabric, dotted with tiny, winking pearls, wind around her hips.

I have to see the back of this confection designed to make a man drag his tongue and lose his mind.

Without warning, I yank her to her feet, tear the skirt from her body, and spin her around to bend her over the island.

Two wide strips of nearly transparent lace stretch from each hip down, lovingly cupping her sweet ass, then disappear into the musky shadow between her legs. From the highest point at each side of the undergarment, silky ribbons entwine like the strings on a corset, playing peekaboo with the cheeks of her ass.

I can't think of a sexier sight than Ella Hope wearing nothing but a tease and a smile.

"Holy fuck."

"I like lingerie." Her shaky voice almost sounds defensive. "Buying it is my guilty pleasure."

"I'm glad." Does she realize just how thoroughly I'm going to fuck her until she can't move, can't think, and can't imagine ever leaving my bed? "And you have more like this?"

"A suitcase full. Some racier."

I grin. This might be the best surprise ever.

I smooth my hand down her spine, over the small of her back, and cup her ass possessively. When she gasps, I smile. Oh, she has no idea what I plan to do to her luscious body.

But I'm about to show her.

"Your hands are hot on my skin." Her whisper is choppy and soft.

Yeah, she's aroused.

I skim my palm around her hip to touch the wings of her protective butterfly. The closer I ease to her center, the damper her lace is.

"And your pussy is wet under my fingers," I mutter in her ear.

Her back arches. Her breath catches. She gives me a jagged nod. "I'm on fire."

I grip both of her hips and align my distended dick with her crease, pressing into her ass as much as her panties and my slacks allow. I deeply resent my zipper. I'd give anything to be stripped down and gloved up right now so I could simply slide inside her and feel just how tight, wet, and ready Ella is for me.

Instead, I grip her hair in my fist. "Tell me what you like."

"E-Everything you're doing."

"I haven't done anything yet."

She lets out a breath and wriggles her hips, twisting against my cock, pressing forward, futilely seeking some relieving pressure from the edge of the island. "You've done more to excite me than I've ever imagined."

Smiling, I bend to press kisses across her shoulder and up the crook of her neck before I nip at her lobe. "I'm going to do so much more."

Without giving her time to speculate what, I slip my hand under her blouse and skim my way up her soft stomach. I need to reach her bra. I need to feel the garment so I can imagine it. And figure out how best to get it off.

My fingers trace the lace-coated underwire, then I flatten my palm to cradle the weight of her breast in my hand. Her flesh fills most of my wide palm. I'm stunned by not only that but the fact there's no fabric covering her nipples. The silky draping of her blouse disguised everything well. "Oh, sweetheart."

I'm a boob man. I don't deny it. And when I whip my free hand up to her other breast and cradle them both in my palms, I realize she's really damn gifted...and I'm so fucking lucky.

Ella tosses her head back to my shoulder. "Carson..."

She's begging for something. Pleasure. Pain. Ecstasy. I pinch her nipples between my thumbs and forefingers. She hisses from clenched teeth and writhes back against me once more.

"If you value that blouse, I suggest you get it off now."

"Y-Yes."

I don't know whether she means she wants the blouse intact or whether she wants me to rip it off. But I feel her fingers tugging at the garment. It goes slack around my arms still shoved underneath. Her fingers brush mine. Then suddenly the sides flutter away from her body, and I yank it free.

The two little straps of her white bra stretch over her shoulders. Three hooks hold everything in place along the back. But I want to see the front. I want to see the little candy points I'm about to have in my mouth unfettered by fabric. I want them bare.

I skim my lips over her ear. "Turn around, Ella. Show me your nipples."

She nods slowly, her breathing picking up pace. "Then you'll take your pants off and fuck me?"

"Sweetheart, I may only wait long enough to unzip." I'll worry about taking them off later.

With a sigh that sounds as if she's relieved, she draws her shoulders up, wrapping her arms around herself, as she twists around in the limited space I've allowed her between the island and my body. When the edge of the counter is tucked into the small of her back, she glances her way from my pecs and up my neck, lingering on my mouth, before meeting my stare. She's got each of her hands wrapped around her opposite elbows, arms covering her nipples. But the cleavage is insane.

"Ella..." I warn. "Show me."

She licks her lips. "You want to see now?"

"Yes."

"You want to touch me?"

"Yes," I growl.

"You want to taste me?"

She's taunting, and I love the way she draws everything out, makes me impatient with the heat and the need to have her. I'm sweating. I can't remember ever wanting a woman the way I must have this one right fucking now.

I grab her wrists. "Move your arms to your sides or I'll do it for you."

Slowly, she releases her elbows. Her palms skim across her forearms, still pressed against her breasts. Just when I'm sure she's going to show me everything, she covers her mounds with her palms. The idea of her being able to hide her spilling flesh behind her small hands is laughable and so fucking arousing I feel as if I'm about to lose my mind.

But she's enjoying the tease. She wants to torment me, make me crazy for her. I want to let her. I'm so jacked up on desire right now it's like a drug jetting through my bloodstream. I can almost see every flutter of her lashes, hear each one of her jerky inhalations, feel all the goose bumps on her skin.

"You sure you really want to see?"

I grunt. "I can count down from three or just take you now. Your choice."

I'm calling her bluff. I'm limiting her options. I'm letting her know I'm at the end of my rope.

"Count," she whispers with a tempting grin.

"Three..."

She presses a kiss to my jaw, then runs her tongue down my neck, to my shoulder, where she sinks her teeth in. Then she soothes that little spot with her tongue. I have no idea why that turns me the fuck on, but I have to drag in a deep breath and lock my fingers around her waist to keep myself from lifting her and impaling her in the next heartbeat.

"Go on."

"Two..."

I'm already holding my breath, wondering what the hell she's going to do to me next, but she doesn't keep me guessing for long. Her lips trail up my neck, to my chin, then to the corner of my lips, where she presses light kisses all around my mouth...but never directly against it, where I need her most.

"Yes," she breathes against my skin.

I swallow hard. "One..."

"Ready or not, here you come?" She taunts me as her hands leave her plump breasts, exposing blushing pink nipples above a naughty quarter bra I barely have time to appreciate before she braces her hands on the counter behind her and lifts herself up, spreading her legs and hooking her heels on the edge.

I gape for a long moment, drinking her in, watching her breasts rise and fall with every panting breath. Then I snap out of it.

"You better fucking believe it." I reach in my wallet for my emergency condom I haven't needed for months, then chuck the billfold and the wrapper on the counter behind me. Then with one hand, I lower my pants. With the other, I caress my way up her thigh, then hook my finger inside those minuscule, tease-me panties.

Jesus, she's soaked.

I want that. I want her. I want to taste her, fuck her, own her. Right now, I don't ever want space between us again. I just want her and me and an endless amount of time to explore every pale, satin curve she's exposed to me.

A little moan escapes her when I graze her clit. It's hard. She's definitely ready.

I should be a gentleman, wait, and give her a few orgasms with my fingers and tongue. And I will. Oh, believe me, that's on my agenda. But right now...

With one deft hand, I roll the condom over my cock. "I need to fuck you. Take your panties off."

They're delicate and complicated, and as juiced up as I am for her now, I know they'll dissolve in my hands if I try to remove them.

"No time," she insists with a frantic shake of her head as she reaches up and slips a fingertip under the front butterfly and pulls it aside, exposing most of her slick folds.

Her pussy is bare.

Ella just keeps getting better and sweeter. If I could have conjured up a woman who tripped every trigger in my body and made me ache for long nights of sweaty, amazing sex, I would have pictured this one. I've always been partial to brunettes. I love her big eyes, big tits, big sense of sexual adventure.

"Good thinking," I praise as I part her folds with one hand and align the head of my cock to her opening with the other. "You sure you're ready?"

She wriggles on my crest until it dips just inside her. "Why? Are you worried you're not?"

I have to smile at her taunt. I'm more fucking aroused than I've ever been, and still she doesn't stop tempting me. She's not grasping the fact that she's created a beast who will happily spend the next forty-eight hours inside her wringing one orgasm after another from her and still be greedy for more.

"Don't say I didn't warn you."

In one move, I grip her hips, lift her against me, and impale her on my cock. My tug and good old gravity work magic. Seconds later, I'm buried deep inside the sweetest clinging, fluttering, gripping pussy ever. She gasps as she steadies herself on my shoulders, hanging on for dear life. All that's great. More than spectacular, actually. But when she raises her head to me, her big black lashes lifting so she can drink me in and her lips parting in an electric moment before our stares meet? Shit, the connection reaches into my chest and squeezes hard. It does the same to my balls. This isn't a simple screw. This isn't a normal fling. She's doing way more than scratching my itch.

Fuck, I could fall for this woman.

I don't know how or why I'm sure that's true. We're barely acquainted with one another. But that knowledge is simmering in my brainpan. I don't doubt it any more than I doubt my ability to spell my name or recite my date of birth.

Ella Hope could be lethal to my heart. And that still doesn't stop me from digging my fingers into her hips and arching up into her body and squeezing another inch into her tight clasp.

"Carson..."

The way she whimpers my name is the sexiest sound I've ever heard.

"Feel good, sweetheart?"

"Yes." She wriggles against me, clenching, adjusting, gyrating with a frown like she's dealing with a torment just shy of pain. "I need—"

"Friction?"

She wraps her arms around my neck, breathing hard against my lips. "You."

Somehow, whatever is happening between us has gone from teasing to dead fucking serious with one thrust. Now that I'm inside her, I don't know how I'm ever going to leave. That's provided I'm ever going to want to.

I cup my hands under her ass and lift her up every one of my aching inches. The drag of my sensitive skin through her wet flesh has me gritting my teeth to hold myself together. Fuck me, this woman is going to undo me fast.

"You got me." I brace my palms on her hips and yank her down every electrified inch of my dick again. "All of me."

As I bottom out, her head falls back. Her mouth gapes open. A high-pitched wail falls out. My neighbors are probably getting one hell of a passionate soundtrack to their evening conversation, and I don't give a shit.

Ella wraps her legs around my middle and digs her fingers, nails and all, into my shoulders. As I lift her up for another thrust, she tries to help, clenching her thighs and using the leverage of all her limbs to work up my throbbing shaft. It's so good...but I need more of her now. Faster. Harder. Deeper. What I don't need is her help.

At the apex of her rise, I slam her back down every inch of me. I don't give her time to adjust or react before I do it again. Again. And again.

Fuck me, after a handful of strokes, the pleasure is beginning to overwhelm. The tight clasp of her is unraveling my control. I could go blind from this pleasure. I grit my teeth to stave off the growing, gnawing ache. Ella doesn't make it easier when she presses those amazing breasts against my chest, brushes kisses over my jaw, then makes her way to my ear.

"God, that's so good…" she moans in my ear. "You're big inside me. I have to stretch to take you, and it's the best kind of burn. The ache behind my clit is hot and growing. I don't know how long I'll last. Carson…"

Holy shit, she just keeps getting sexier. Her body gives me so many clues about her arousal, but her words…yeah. That's the icing on top of the sweet confection of her body that's already so smooth and melting on my tongue.

"Don't hold back for me," I insist. "I'll fuck you through every orgasm, sweetheart, and start giving you another one in the next instant. But this tight little pussy is mine to pleasure, to use…" *To own.*

I raise her to the tip of my cock again, then shuttle her back down, reveling in her response that's somewhere between a breathy gasp and a strangled whimper. And there she is, tightening around me even more, breathing harder, nails digging in farther.

Under that button-down blouse and her professional exterior beats the heart of a temptress. This really isn't a great time in my life to start thinking with my dick, but that's not going to stop me. I've been around the block enough to have memorized all the usual speed bumps—drama queens, narcissists, gold diggers, clinging vines, Madonnas, whores, girls with daddy issues... You name it. Ella seems like a woman I can simply be myself with.

When I drag her down my cock again, a groan tears from my chest. I'm on fire. I want deeper. I need her under me. I have to take every part of her in every way. Right now.

Laying her flat against the island again, I watch as her eyes flare. She hisses and her body bows at the cool granite chilling her back, but this position leaves her legs spread, pussy open, clit exposed. I look down at her flushed face, dazed eyes, and breasts that bounce with every thrust—and I know I won't be able to hold out much longer.

Caressing my way up her thigh as I bend my knees just enough to take another long, deep glide through her slick flesh—and dragging against her most sensitive spot—I settle my thumb over her clit and rub in small circles.

Her body tenses. She grips the edge of the counter. And then she screams my name in a wail of impending climax. "Carson!"

She's close, and I'm so attuned to her that the tension mounting in her body is the same tension gripping mine. I flick my thumb over her distended bud faster, watching her mouth fall open, the flush spread across her chest, her nipples harden to steel points.

"Ella." Her name is a groan that rips from my throat. I swallow. I have more to say, more to demand of her, but the ecstasy begins to swarm my head. Everything except her and the orgasm we're about to share fades away.

This woman turns me on like no one. It's been months since I've relished sex, and I've never felt as if I could plunge into one woman, anchor myself deep, and stay forever. Pleasure brews in my blood, tingles at the base of my cock, and rushes to the head, especially when she claws at me and clamps around me so tight I can barely move.

Oh, shit. There's no stopping the freight train of this pounding satisfaction.

As I manipulate her clit with swirling strokes using the last of my sanity, her entire body arches and jolts. A scream spills from her pouting lips. Her pussy clenches and releases, gripping me unrelentingly.

That's it. I can't wait. Pleasure jets as I grip the far side of the island above her head and surge into her roughly over and over until I'm coming with her, emptying myself of weeks of grief, stress, and uncertainty. I pour into Ella, leaving a part of myself inside her. As my strokes slow, peace steals over me, and my heartbeat seems to sync up with hers.

Our breathing slows and our eyes meet. Something in my chest clutches.

"What just happened?" She asks exactly the question I was thinking.

The best sex of my life? I swallow the simple answer. None of this feels simple at all.

"No idea," I manage to mutter.

A warning voice in my head tells me I should withdraw—literally and figuratively—and keep our relationship to exactly what we agreed to on paper before Ella ever stepped foot on the plane. But she wraps her arms around my neck and settles her pillowy mouth over my lips for a lingering kiss, and I fear very much that option is off the table for good.

"Me neither. But I think we should do it again." She gives me a sly smile. "You know, just to study it."

The monumental orgasm I had three minutes ago is a memory when I feel my cock stirring again. How is that even possible?

"Food first?" I ask.

Maybe reheating and eating will give me some time to wrap my head around why this woman seems to make an impact on me that's on par with a mile-wide meteor.

She wriggles underneath me. "I vote for later. You got round two in you?"

Her voice is a challenge I can't not respond to. "Oh, yeah."

Ella gives me a mischievous grin as she wraps her legs around my middle even tighter. "Then I want you to take me to bed and not let me up until morning."

Smart or not, it's so on.

"All right," I growl as I kick out of my pants. Then I lift her from the island and walk with our bodies still entwined across the apartment, kicking the bedroom door shut behind me. "And come tomorrow, when you're hungry, exhausted, and sore, I want you to remember that I gave you exactly what you asked for."

ELLA

"Seriously?" I ask just before Carson forks another warm bite of tender fillet into my mouth. I shouldn't be relishing this...but I do. The juice. The flavor. The way he takes care of me...

"I said I was going to feed you." His voice teases and chides me at once. "Sit back and let me do it."

With a sigh of surrender, I lean into the stack of pillows at the head of the rumpled bed. After hours of amazing, spine-tingling, downright athletic sex, I don't have the energy to do anything but open my mouth and let him have his way. As I dozed off for a few minutes, he disappeared, only to return with a tray of steaming food. I have no idea how he reheated everything from the steakhouse to perfection, but the orgasmic bliss he sent humming through my body earlier has now made its way to my satisfied tongue.

"I assumed you meant that you were going to take me out for a meal, not hand-feed me every morsel."

He shakes his head. "You know the old saying about assumptions?"

I know quite well. I won't make the same mistake about jumping to conclusions with Carson Frost again. "Touché. You really don't have to personally lift each bite to my mouth."

"But this way, I know you're actually eating." He dips the fork into the potatoes au gratin and lifts it again with a steamy, cheesy heap. "And I'm enjoying it."

My head tells me to demand that he stop now...but my taste buds are having a party. I've been living on kale salads, vegetable smoothies, and grilled chicken for years. Besides, Carson and I have been so busy, we must have burned off at least a thousand calories. Not to mention the fact that I've never had such an attentive lover. "In all honesty, I'm enjoying this, too."

He gives me an indulgent smile. "Seriously, you have no reason to watch your weight."

"I appreciate that. The truth is, my drama coach in college told me that, at my height, if I ever weighed more than a hundred and ten, I would never make it big. Sadly, my experiences have proven her right." I've actually been fighting my body since puberty. Short of starvation or a strictly liquid diet, my frame simply refuses to shed much weight. I always carry about twenty pounds more than I want. Some days, I'm exhausted by the never-ending battle.

So, after a dozen years of frustration and deprivation, the indulgence Carson is sliding onto my tongue is a downright thrill.

"Want me to open a bottle of wine?"

With sleepy eyes, I slide a glance over at the clock. "It's almost three in the morning. Aren't you tired?"

He shovels some of the steak into his mouth, followed by a forkful of potatoes. Then he unwraps another covered dish, and the scent of the lobster macaroni and cheese almost has me swooning.

"A little. But between you and our amazing leftovers, I'm getting my second wind. It's only midnight for you, West Coast girl. What's your excuse?"

I laugh. "I'm usually in bed by ten so I can be ready for early morning auditions. You've kept me up a lot longer."

Carson lifts the sheet away from his lap, then shoves it aside. His cock—every bit as big as my toes discovered—is standing tall. "You're keeping me up, too."

I can't believe he's hard again...and I can't say I'm unhappy about it.

"Are you always this insatiable?" I've barely finished the question before he's plying my taste buds with the creamy, soft goodness of the macaroni. I bite into a chunk of the lobster and moan.

"No. That's all you," he says solemnly.

"That's amazing..."

He quirks a golden brow at me. "My stamina?"

"That, too. But I meant the orgasm in the takeout tin over there."

When I laugh, he does the same. "Well, I've got more—of whatever you want."

Then he sets about tugging at the sheet covering my naked breasts, exposing my well-loved nipples and the flesh slightly rosy from orgasmic glow and whisker burn.

"I'll keep that in mind," I promise with a catch of my breath.

He sets his food aside for a moment, then leans in to kiss my lips, my neck, my shoulder, the swell of my breast... My eyes slide shut for a luxurious moment. I know where this is headed. We still haven't managed more than a few bites of food. We haven't retrieved my suitcase from the car yet, either.

I slide a hand between my flesh and his mouth before he can suck my nipple and make me lose my mind. "You promised to feed me before you tumble me to the bed again. And didn't we discuss a shower?"

Carson grimaces and backs away. "Yeah. Sorry. I lose my head with you. I have to be in a meeting in five hours. And right now, I just don't care."

"You should. You've done a lot to save Sweet Darlin'," I point out. "But you surprise me. You're not as driven as I thought when we first talked."

"What do you mean? I'm ambitious."

He is. If he weren't, he never would have assumed the helm of Sweet Darlin' or found himself engaged to Kendra Shaw. "But you're not the kind of workaholic who forgets there's another person in the room. You're not the sort to disregard the people around you."

At that observation, he scowls. "Have you dated someone like that? If so, he sounds like a terrible prick."

In a weird way, that's actually sweet of him to say. Normally, I wouldn't share much about my past with a boss or a date. But Carson is different. "No. I'm talking about my parents. My dad was a reporter for the ABC affiliate in Los Angeles. My mom was a costume designer who worked for various TV shows. They both worked incredibly long hours. When Dad was home at all, he was forever on the phone or leaving in the middle of dinner to meet an informant or chase a crime scene. Mom was around more, but she always had her head stuck in a sketchbook or was cozying up to her sewing machine. Sometimes, my younger sisters and I felt invisible."

His face softens. "I'm sorry. My mom and stepdad had their faults—they were human, after all—but they were great parents. I know how it feels to be invisible and irrelevant, though. I spent a lot of time growing up wondering why my own dad never wanted me, why my mom had to marry someone else to find a guy who gave a shit about me."

I nod. It seems as if he truly does understand. "I had to become an adult to realize that my parents weren't awful or uncaring or neglectful on purpose. They simply picked occupations they were so passionate about that sometimes they would forget everything else. In some ways, they saw the work they did as a public service. My dad gave truth to the community. My mom added beauty and authenticity to the world."

"But it would have been nice if they'd remembered to be parents more often, too, right?"

I nod. "Exactly. I can't complain much. I grew up in a nice house, went to good schools, had awesome friends. No one beat me. I never went hungry. I shouldn't complain."

"But everyone wants to be loved," he says softly.

Maybe I'm just tired. Or maybe my emotions are raw because in the last few hours, this man has opened my body to him in nearly every conceivable way. All I know is that my eyes well with stinging tears.

"Yeah." I sniffle, determined to lighten the suddenly heavy mood. "And love in return, so could you give me another forkful of those heavenly potatoes?"

With an understanding smile, he hands me the round tin and my fork, then sets about inhaling his own dinner. "God, everything tastes amazing. I was starved."

"I was, too." Not just for the food but for the toe-curling sex, affection, and understanding.

We both eat up, and I decide that I'm just not worrying about calories anymore today. He'll go to work in a few hours, and I'll pay penance with a lean breakfast, a long stretch of yoga, and a good hour on the stationary bike I noticed in the corner.

Finally, we both finish scarfing down our steaks and all our side dishes with gusto. Once we're done, Carson groans and lies back on the bed, wrapping his hand around my ankle and skating his fingers up and down my calf. "This is the happiest I've been since I moved here. I gave up all my friends and dived into a company I only had a passing knowledge about. Half the management staff has been against me from the minute I walked in the door, and I don't have just cause to fire them. So I've had to work hard to slowly change their minds. Juggling everything has been a bitch and a half."

"It sounds like a lot of work. Did one of the existing executives want to assume responsibility of the company?" I shrug. "If so, why not let them?"

"Because my biological father's last wish was for me to take the reins. Part of me wonders if he did that in death because he wasn't with me in life. A few of my friends said that sounded like wishful thinking. Maybe it is. But this company meant everything to him. Now that I've been here almost six months, I understand. Think about the number of people who enjoy their candy with a favorite movie or fill their kids' Easter baskets or eat something Sweet Darlin' has cooked up because it reminds them of their own childhoods. I get mail every day from average people and employees alike who thank me for not letting their favorite treats die with my biological father. My cousin Jagger ran the organization for a few months, between Edward's catastrophic head injury and the day he was removed from life support. He was cutting costs because that's what he learned you should do in the one junior college business administration class he'd taken, but that meant he was cutting quality and employee pay. He didn't know anything about running an organization, much less one this size. When I figured out what he'd done, I was angry on my biological dad's behalf. I didn't know Edward well, but I've learned a lot about the man he must have been by reading his notes, files, and correspondence. I understand how he would have wanted Sweet Darlin' run, so that's what I'm doing."

I admire Carson all the more for it. I know how easy it would have been to be bitter toward the parent who hadn't spared you any time as a kid. But he's risen above it and given himself a new purpose. "I'm sure you've made him very happy. What you've done can't be easy. Between the grief of losing the man you'll never know well and the responsibility he left behind, a lot of people would have caved already."

He gives me a thoughtful nod. "It's been a lot of effort. I haven't taken a day off in months. But tonight, being here with you...this has been everything I've needed. Thanks, Ella."

"Stop. You're making me blush," I tease him.

Then a sly grin creases his face. "I can do more to make you blush, sweetheart. Come here..."

That voice I now know so well makes me tremble. It's deep and low. It's full of mischief and possession and sin. "What if I refuse?"

I can't resist teasing this man. Taunting him. Tempting him. In response, he delivers the sexiest threats. We fell into this pattern so quickly and easily, and I'm addicted to knowing that I can start unraveling this big man with nothing more than my words, my voice, my expression. It's a turn-on. Heck, *he's* a turn-on. All I want is more.

"I'll make you come here, little girl. And once I get you where I want you, I'll make your torment so much worse..."

I roll closer to him, press our torsos together, and throw my leg over his. "Is that so?"

He glides a hand down my body, starting at my shoulder and working his way to my back and over my ass, cupping one cheek and bringing me closer. "Yes. Did I stutter?"

"Not at all." I grin at him. "But you're still feeling me up instead of getting busy, so I can only guess that you're not really serious. What a shame..."

"Are you're challenging me, woman?"

"Maybe." My smile widens. "Does that make you quake in your

boots?"

"First, I don't have any boots," he growls. "Second, if you're serious, sweetheart, I'm so ready."

My playful expression turns completely smug because he's going to give me exactly what I want...except he doesn't. Instead, he bounds off the bed and marches out the bedroom door. "Carson?"

"Get ready," he calls as he retreats.

I hear a drawer open and close in the kitchen, followed by an electronic beep of the oven. What is he doing? The clatter of plates tells me nothing. As I hear him stomping back to the bedroom, I sit up and push my tangled tresses from my face. I already caught sight of myself in a mirror earlier. Ugh. There's a reason people call it "sex hair."

"For what?"

No answer.

I smell heaven before I see it. A moment later, Carson struts through the door stark naked—which, believe me, is a to-die-for view on its own—carrying a plate piled with the bread pudding he ordered at the steakhouse. It's covered in creamy sauce. It almost looks like vanilla, but the slight caramel tinge and smell of hazelnut tell me it's way more amazing.

"Are we going to eat that in bed?"

He sends me a challenging glance. "No. I'm going to eat this off your body. Lie back."

I shouldn't like his bossiness or his commanding tone. But right now, I do. In fact, I feel as if I'm flushing from head to toe and my heart is chugging pure anticipation through my bloodstream.

"All right," I murmur as he sets the plate on the nightstand, yanks out a condom, and rolls it down his still-impressive length. Will I ever stop wriggling when I see him eager and ready?

"You're not moving," he points out. "I'm waiting. Or is this just too adventurous for you?"

His smirk and his taunt tug me from my visual pleasure and get me focusing on what comes next. I drape myself across the bed and part my legs enough to tease him. "Of course not. This what you had in mind?"

He simply smiles and stabs the fork into the middle of the bread pudding, heaping it onto the tines. The warm sauce drips on my thigh and hip as he lifts the dessert toward my chest. He unloads it in the valley of my cleavage, reaches for the plate again, and retrieves a smaller bite.

"What are you doing?"

He cups the back of my head with one hand and lifts me enough to meet the fork waiting with a scrumptious bite in the other. I open my mouth and let him slide the dessert onto my tongue because this looks like the kind of epic sugar concoction that will never cross my lips again. One bite can't hurt that much, right?

"I'm feeding you before I feed *on* you."

My taste buds are in ecstasy. It melts on my tongue, dissolving into a cloud of pure delight, moistened by the creamy, rich sauce that's sunken into every nook and cranny and made the consistency something close to heaven. I moan, and it's not ladylike or delicate. This is a full-on groan of utter bliss. "That is *amazing*!"

"Glad to hear it. But I'm not going to take your word for it, Ella."

Those words might have been slightly ominous if he didn't break off part of the warm dessert nestled between my breasts and smear it over my nipples. The warmth hits my sensitive flesh first. It's sticky, and if you had asked me yesterday if I wanted Carson Frost to smear stale baked bread mixed with liqueur all over my boobs, I would have laughed before I answered with a big *hell no*. But in these amazing hours before dawn, the only thing that seems important is the way we make each other feel. If he wants to eat off my body, I'm more than game. I'm excited.

In the back of my head, I realize I'm giving him a lot of myself, and that in a little over two weeks I'll be packing up and heading home, probably never to see this man again. But that's *so* seventeen days from now, and I have a suspicion we have a lot more pleasure to find together. When this assignment is over, maybe the glow I'm feeling with this surprising attachment will have dimmed. After all, what are the chances that the guy who hired me to jilt him would be my soul mate? And...I admit it, everything between us now feels too damn good to stop.

For Carson, I arch my back and lift my breasts to him. "I don't think you should take my word for it. Why skip dessert when you've gone to all this trouble?"

With a snarl that lights me up, he pounces on me, practically inhaling my breast. With a low groan, he thoroughly licks it up one side, then drags his lips back down the other. He circles my nipple a few times, inching closer and closer to the aching tip without actually touching it. A whimper escapes my throat.

"Impatient, sweetheart?"

"Yes. Hurry, Carson." In the fuzzy part of my brain, it occurs to me that, as much as he enjoys toying with me, he's not going to give me what I want simply because I whine for it. He's going to make me suffer, make me wait. He'll make me earn it.

I'd never admit this aloud, but I wouldn't want it any other way.

"But you have another breast covered in bread pudding that I haven't even touched. You can't expect me to rush through this. Dessert is the best part of any meal."

He shifts his attention to my other mound, nibbling around my sensitive crest, laving my flesh as he increases my ache. I wriggle restlessly, but he won't let up. He eats away at his dessert in an unhurried savoring that's breaking down my composure. I really didn't think he could arouse me again this much tonight. I lost count of the number of orgasms he's already given me. I was certain I was totally sated.

I was wrong.

Finally, he decides he wants the next part of his sexy sugarfest, so he leans in and drags his tongue over one nipple, then the other, before sucking each deep onto his tongue in an unhurried, alternating rhythm. I gasp at the feel of his hot mouth enveloping me and frantically grab for strands of his short hair, trying to hang on to this seemingly endless descent into pleasure. It's astonishing, the things he makes me feel. I never believed my nipples were sensitive until now. I never thought marathon sex was my thing, either. I have a bad feeling Carson has forever changed that—and me.

Once he's licked clean all traces of the bread pudding, except one last heap between my breasts, he starts shifting his way down my body, dragging his lips as he sidles his way between my legs.

Oh, my god. I'm so aroused now that if he puts his mouth down there, I'm going to explode. "Carson..."

"You have to stop trying to come between a man and his dessert, sweetheart," he teases.

Before I have time to say another word, he scoops up the last of the sugary-cakey goodness and spreads it across the pad of my pussy. Then he burrows his arms under my thighs and lifts my hips until my slit is inches from his mouth.

And he waits, licking his lips, staring at me with hungry blue eyes.

He wants me to offer myself to him or beg or something that I would normally never do. But Carson can wring me inside out sexually and make me behave in ways I normally wouldn't.

Panting, my heart a harsh thud against my chest, I spread my legs a little wider. "You're right. I should let you thoroughly enjoy everything you find sweet..."

With a shark's grin, he nods. "I intend to."

Then, as if words now bore him, Carson stops talking and starts feasting. At first he does nothing but lick the soft bread pudding from the apex above my slit. I feel the gentle nip of his teeth on the fleshy part of my pussy, my skin slicked by Frangelico and my own juices. But inevitably, he delves lower, sliding first his fingers, then the tip of his tongue over the hard button of my clit. It's throbbing before he ever makes direct contact, and by the time he sucks it into his mouth to savor the last of his dessert, I'm squealing in delight, nearly bolting off the bed—and rocketing to an orgasm that blows my mind.

The last of the pulses have barely finished when he shimmies up my body, lips and fingers busy, then slams inside me completely, stealing my breath and wrapping himself around my heart as if he means to make away with that, too.

It's too late to try resisting the pull between us. The time for that would have been before dessert. Hell, before I even got off the plane. This man is definitely going to be dangerous to my peace of mind and my skittish heart. And right now, he's filling every space inside me, scraping my nerve endings and my emotions raw. I can't seem to do anything but let the inevitable happen. My need climbs. His thrusts quicken. Our passion swells. He's going to give me another head-spinning climax. I can feel it coming...

And I can't do anything to stop the fact that he'll take my soul with it.

Even knowing the truth, I open to him, wrap my arms around him, and give him everything. If he decides there's nothing meaningful between us at the end of this job, I'll at least know I couldn't have tried harder to give him every part of myself.

That's my last thought before pleasure rips me open, bursting wide, leaving me utterly exposed and bleeding out love.

CHAPTER FIVE

CARSON

Early Friday morning, I roll away from another ground-shaking orgasm with Ella, panting and staring at the ceiling and wondering— not for the first time—if I ever want her to go back to LA.

She melts against my side, hot cheek lying on my chest, hand splayed between my pecs. "Wow..."

"Yeah. Holy shit." I kiss the top of her head.

In fact, I can't not touch her in some way if I'm in a room with her. I can't even stand not talking to her if she's nearby. In the last two days, I've developed a ritual that begins with cuddling with her when I first wake while we talk about our day. Eventually, that leads to sex because...well, when doesn't something between us lead to sex? Then I call her from the car. I text her between meetings. I even ring her if someone has pissed me off at work. She's always there. She always listens. She always offers empathy and good advice.

How am I supposed to do without all that when she returns to starving herself in a sea of shallow people in Southern California?

"We have to actually get a whole night's sleep at some point," she murmurs tiredly.

"Yeah. And probably a whole meal."

She laughs. "We have been a little too impatient for food lately, haven't we?"

When she lifts her gaze to me and our eyes meet, I swear I see her heart in her eyes. I feel that *zing* again. I've been feeling it since the night she arrived. Sometimes, I'm sure she feels it, too. I have a sneaking suspicion I know what's brewing between us because every day, every time our stares tangle, it gets stronger.

I run a freaking billion-dollar company. I managed to hold off my wily business rival who's also my prospective father-in-law with some quick words and a well-placed lie. Just yesterday, I verbally eviscerated a greedy supplier and one of my over-anxious creditors on the phone, no problem.

But I can't seem to find the right words to ask Ella how she feels about me.

"I have to go to work." I disentangle myself from her soft curves and leave her sprawled and naked on the bed as I head to the shower. But walking away is a fight.

Not surprisingly, she follows me, caressing her way down my back. "You all right?"

"Yeah. Just a lot on my mind." And not about the things I should be worrying over.

"Anything I can help with?"

I'm really tempted to say something. In fact, I know I should. It's stupid to be insecure about her feelings if I don't bother to ask, and the fact that she even wants to listen to me says something. But is that about her attachment to me or her general compassion as a human being?

I start the water in the shower, trying to get my head on straight, and change the subject. "Kendra texted me yesterday."

Ella tenses. "What did she say? Has she started school yet?"

"Not until Monday. But Greek activities have already started and she's been busy with those. She asked me how things were going with you. And apparently, she met a guy who's involved in ROTC. He wants to be a naval officer." I sigh. "They had coffee together last night. He asked her out tomorrow."

She pauses. "How do you feel about that?"

"Relieved. I told her she should date him. I don't want to hurt her, but I don't want to marry her. She doesn't want to marry me, either. But she can't be the one to end our engagement or she loses millions. Ditto here." I shake my head. "One of us will have to flinch first."

"We'll figure it out. I'm here to help, remember? What you need is to convince Shaw to take an interest in Sweet Darlin' without making you and Kendra both miserable."

"I've tried, but maybe if you and I are convincing tonight, he'll relent and let the deal proceed without this stupid corporate wedding. I don't know. When he told me to bring the woman I'd fallen for, he was calling my bluff. So I suspect he'll have some scheme up his sleeve. He isn't the sort of man to go down without a fight."

"Don't worry about it now. Focus on your day. We'll deal with the rest as it comes at the benefit tonight."

"Thanks, sweetheart." The words fall off my tongue. I'm struck by how much we sound like a real couple. I talk. She listens. We exchange ideas and a touch and...life continues.

I reach for the shower door since I see steam filming the clear glass. I expect Ella will put on her short blue robe and head to the kitchen to make something both healthy and protein-based that I'll pretend to complain about but actually enjoy. Then I'll kiss her and head off to the office and spend my day wishing I were with her. She hasn't even left the room yet and I already miss her.

Instead, she enters the shower behind me.

"Do you mind?" she asks as she eases against me, sliding her water-slick skin over mine.

"That you're here with me?" I shake my head. "Not at all."

Ella's smile is sunny as she wraps her arms around my neck and kisses me softly.

I wrap her in my arms, caress the soft line of her spine, skate my palms down to the curve of her hips, and drag her closer.

Again, I can't help but wonder where this is heading. My life is here, and hers is in Los Angeles. My head knows that, but I've been subconsciously imagining our future together—and trying to figure out if I can make it a reality. Yes, Gregory Shaw worries me. If I don't play this right, he can crush me in his fist. But that isn't my only consideration.

The stark reality is, there's nothing for me on the West Coast anymore except some friends and memories. Mom and Craig are gone, my childhood home sold. On the other hand, what's in North Carolina for Ella except me? I can't ask this woman to give up her dreams. She lights up when she talks about them.

The smart thing to do would be to get through tonight, then put distance between me and the "girlfriend" I'm paying. Turn away the sex, shut off the emotion, toss up a mental wall or two.

When it comes to Ella, I don't know if I can be smart.

"Tell me something. What's your fallback plan?" I ask her. "If you never make a living at acting, what else would you want to do with your life?"

She cocks her head. "I'd probably teach drama and theater to kids. I did a few camps last summer with children hand-selected from their respective schools as the brightest and most talented. We put on a couple of small productions throughout the summer and ended the session with *A Midsummer Night's Dream*. They really enjoyed it, and it was so rewarding to work with youngsters who have their whole lives ahead of them and such amazing voices and theatric gifts."

"That sounds great." I rinse my head under the spray and give her words some thought.

A camp like that is something she could do anywhere. And the glow on her face when she's talking about molding kids and helping to shape their futures hits me square in the chest. It takes me a moment, but I realize why. I want to make Ella Hope happy, and her memories of last summer very clearly do.

Any chance she would be happy here with me, teaching kids how to develop their inner thespian?

Maybe, but after two days with this woman, I'm getting way ahead of myself. I'm on the verge of asking her to give up her life in California, her potential stardom, and whatever else she's got going on out there for me—a man who can't seem to work up the courage to tell her that he might be falling in love with her.

"It was really rewarding. I took the job because it gave me some great connections and a steady paycheck for a few months. But I think I got way more out of it than that."

"You'd be great with kids."

Her face softens. "Every one of them deserves attention and praise, and after my own upbringing..."

She feels compelled to make every child feel important and valued. It's something I admire about her. I'm terrible about getting caught up in my day-to-day life. I don't always stop to think about the people around me, what they're going through, what they need. I should be better. Everyone around me should expect it. I'm glad Ella has made me realize it.

"You ever think about settling down, getting married and all that?" I reach for the shampoo like this is a nonchalant conversation.

But my heart is racing.

She shrugs. "Sure, as much as the next girl, I guess. That's definitely in my 'someday' category." Suddenly, she gives me a rueful smile. "But right now, I'll bet you're thinking a lot more about getting married than I am."

Did she read my mind? Does she know that I'm resisting the notion of picturing my future without her? Then I realize she means Kendra.

"Yeah. It's not that I don't want to get married someday. I'm thirty. I think I'd be ready...with the right person for the right reason. Gregory Shaw's sorority-house daughter to cement a business deal isn't it."

"I'm kind of looking forward to meeting her tonight, just to see her for myself."

Kendra will be more than happy to meet her, too. Hell, my supposed fiancée would probably throw the entire line of the Rockettes my way if it would get her out of marrying me.

I finish lathering up my hair, rinse, and grope my way over to the nearby shelf to grab my bottle of shower gel, but it's gone.

Moments later, Ella rubs her palms across my chest, and I inhale the familiar scent of my bodywash as the slick gel spreads over my skin.

"What are you doing, sweetheart?" I groan.

"Sending you off to work with a smile."

She kisses me and lathers my body, then focuses all her attention on my cock, now raging for her touch. One caress, and I swear I feel as if I haven't had her in a century. It's crazy. It's wonderful. It's terrible—especially if this is all just fun and games for her.

I'm lost in a smoldering haze of pleasure that's beginning to build when she plucks the portable showerhead from its holder and rinses me off thoroughly, skimming her teasing touch over every inch of me.

"Can I return the favor?"

"No. I'm not completely sure you're squeaky clean yet. There's just one more spot..."

Then she drops to her knees and takes me into her mouth. I lose my mind—along with the rest of my heart.

As I grip her hair in my fists, dying under the lash of her tongue dancing along the sensitive crest and wrapping down my aching shaft, I let go of my self-control, chiding myself that I either need to tell her I'm falling in love...or let her go for good.

ELLA

Carson is waiting for me on the living room sofa when I step from the bedroom, securing the second of my sparkly earrings. "I'm ready."

He stands and turns—and I see *that* look in his eyes.

"Ella..."

He breathes my name like he's mesmerized, and my pussy clenches. Everything about him has my heart stuttering dangerously.

"You like it?" I hold my arms out wide so he can get a good eyeful of my silvery-gray silk sheath. Its scalloped straps drape over my shoulders. The neckline is scooped deep enough to show my cleavage and the swells of my breasts before it narrows to my waist and flares out to accommodate the rest of my curves. From hip to hem, a band of lace exposes my right side. The dress nips in again at my knees, then spreads gently at the feet one last time like the bell of a trumpet.

Looking incredible in a tuxedo, Carson makes his way to my side. "Like? Wow, you look beyond amazing. Really. Words fail me, sweetheart. I've never seen a woman more beautiful."

I have no idea if he means what he's saying or if he's merely pumping up my ego because he wants me to feel confident before we do battle tonight. Either way, he makes me blush and swoon. "Thanks."

"Thank you. You'll knock Shaw dead." He wraps an arm around me. "You know, we'd send a whole different message if we were fashionably late. Or better yet, if we don't show up at all. Kendra's father already knows you're real. He's seen pictures of us kissing, I'm pretty sure. I could leave him a voice mail that—"

"Stop right there, mister," I cut in, even though I'd twenty times rather stay home with Carson. "First, I took all the effort to get dressed up, so you're taking me out and showing me off. Second..." I take his hand and give it a squeeze. "You owe this to Shaw. Six days ago he gave you a week to introduce me to him. If not now, when?"

Carson sighs heavily, as if he knows that fate and duty have left him little choice. "But I'd rather have you all to myself tonight. Well, every night."

Not for the first time, I wonder if he's just enjoying the sex...or whether this means something more to him, like it does to me. "Well, since you paid me to look pretty and act devoted, not have sex with you—because that would make me a hooker, which I'm totally not—I think we should go. You need to convince Shaw we're in love. He'll loan you the money, then you and Sweet Darlin' will live happily ever after."

He leans in, his gaze snagging mine and delving deep. I feel as if he's trying to tell me something without words. "What if it's more complicated than that, Ella?"

The question comes out so softly. My heart catches as he eases closer and brushes his lips against mine. "Then we figure it out."

He drags in a breath that doesn't sound entirely steady and nods. "Then let's get this over with so we can come back here and shut the rest of the world out."

I should probably be more careful with my heart, but I'm beyond all caution now. How did this happen so fast?

The drive to the hotel is quiet. It's grating on my nerves. I fear Carson is thinking something, but I'm afraid to hope that he and I are on the same page. He's too logical to fall in love in two days, right?

But even if we are thinking the same thoughts, what comes next? He's not leaving Sweet Darlin'. It would be unfair of me to ask him to chuck his father's legacy so I could pursue my very uncertain acting dream, which admittedly may never come true. What if he wanted me to move here with him? Could I give up the support system of my two sisters and all my friends and move to a city I barely know when it will most assuredly end any chance of landing meaningful roles and someday winning an Oscar?

On the other hand, am I prepared to give up Carson?

When we arrive at the hotel where the benefit is being held, the valet opens my door and takes the car. Hand in hand, Carson and I head inside the ballroom. Signs and banners proclaim this a charity event to build schools, daycares, and playgrounds via a Christian charity for underprivileged children.

"This looks like a great cause," I observe, peering at pictures of their charitable work.

Carson nods tersely, already scanning the room. "My dad was the biggest sponsor of this shindig every year. I wanted to continue the tradition, but Gregory Shaw horned in. No doubt, he wants the good publicity."

I refrain from mentioning that even if Edward Frost found this cause immensely satisfying, he probably started it for the positive press, too. Instead, I squeeze his fingers. The closer we've come to the hotel, the more nervous he's become. Is he worried we won't pass Shaw's muster?

I tug on his hand and pull him around to face me. When his gaze falls on me, he seems to relax a bit.

With an encouraging smile, I reach up and straighten his tie. "We're going to be great. Everything will work out fine. I'll convince Shaw. I'm a professional, remember?"

"Yeah." He nods, breathing out the absent reply. "I know."

I frown. "Do you think something will go wrong?"

Carson cups my face. "My concern is so much bigger than that. What's happening between—"

"Hi, Carson," a lilting feminine voice interrupts.

Before me, he stiffens and slowly lets me go, turning to face a gorgeous blonde suddenly beside us. "Kendra. It's good to see you."

"It's good to see you, too," she murmurs as she's looking directly at me with unabashed curiosity. She's also fidgeting like she's antsy.

He dutifully brushes a kiss across her cheek—but never lets go of my hand. "You look lovely."

And she does, wearing a champagne-glitter sheath with tiny spaghetti straps. Her hair is a perfect gold-to-platinum ombré. She's got high cheekbones, glowing skin, a graceful neck, and the kind of delicate beauty that would be a huge hit back home.

A moment of jealousy flares through me until I realize that Carson doesn't look thrilled to see her at all...and she doesn't look any more excited about the idea of spending the evening with him. A glance at her hand reveals she's not wearing her engagement ring.

"You look handsome, too. Dad told me you were bringing your... friend from California. Is this her?" Kendra nods my way.

"Yes. This is Ella Hope. Ella, Kendra."

We exchange a quick smile and an even quicker handshake.

"Good to meet you," she tells me, then turns back to Carson. "Can you and I talk for a minute?"

He shrugs. "Sure."

"Alone, if you don't mind." She gives me an apologetic grimace.

I tense. Kendra is technically his fiancée, and she's stunning. But Carson clearly has zero interest in her. The fact that he hired me at all, along with his less-than-thrilled expression, tells me to sheath my claws.

"Go ahead." I nod. "I'll grab a drink and get the lay of the land."

"We have a reserved table at the front," Carson says. "I'll meet you there shortly."

"Perfect."

I start to walk away, but to my surprise, he brushes a soft kiss on my lips. I wonder what he's trying to say with that gesture. Is it a reassurance for me, a subtle keep-away for Kendra, or simply a show for all?

"I won't be long," he promises.

With a nod, I leave the two of them in peace. I have no idea what Kendra wants, but she seems nervous, uneasy, anxious to talk. Has she changed her mind about wanting to get married? Is she jealous now that she sees Carson with someone else?

I pause at the bar and grab a club soda with a twist of lime, then saunter around the room, looking at all the jumbo screens designed to tear at the heartstrings and open wallets by flashing pictures of underprivileged children. It works. Those sad faces wrench at me. The misery and suffering of youngsters who should be far more innocent hits me right in the heart. I wish I could do something, but I'm flat broke. I'd give them my time and experience...if I lived here.

As I look away from a particularly adorable little girl in a threadbare dress, guilt pummels me.

"You must be Carson's date."

I whirl to the sound of a man's deep voice. The resemblance between father and daughter is too great to mistake. Same narrow face. Same wide-set eyes. Same dripping-in-money aura.

Steeling my expression, I stick my hand out in his direction.

"Ella Hope. I've heard a lot about you, Mr. Shaw. It's nice to meet you."

"I doubt very much you find it nice, Ella." He gives me a tight smile. "You know, when Carson first told me he'd fallen madly for another woman back in California, I didn't believe you even existed. You're beautiful enough. He's got good taste in women, I'll give him that."

Is he sizing me up or hitting on me? "Thank you." I glance around the room to see if I can catch a glimpse of Carson and Kendra. "Where's Mrs. Shaw?"

"She died six years ago. Breast cancer."

His tone is clipped, as if the subject still causes him a great deal of pain. "I didn't know. I'm sorry."

He gives me a gracious nod. "It's not something I talk about often. Neither does Kendra." He glances down at the drink in my hand. "I see you've found libations."

"Yes. I'm looking at all the good work the charity seems to be doing. It's touching and wonderful."

"Hmm," he mutters in a noncommittal tone. "Where are Carson and Kendra?"

Good question. Would a guy supposedly head-over-heels for me leave me alone in a roomful of strangers and take off with another woman, especially one he's engaged to, two minutes after hitting the door? It sounds dubious, and I don't want to arouse Shaw's suspicions. Nor do I want to tell him that, even now, he and Kendra might be hiding in a corner somewhere, plotting the end of their wedding.

I paste on a smile. "When we arrived, I slipped away to the

ladies' room to check my lipstick, so Carson and I got separated. I'm sure he's here somewhere, looking for me. He's very attentive."

"Indeed. Were you surprised when he called and told you how he felt about you?"

We've discussed our cover story more than once, so I'm completely prepared. "Stunned, really. If he looked at me twice when I dated his friend, I wasn't aware of it. But he's a gentleman and would never have risked a friendship. I've known for some time that the other relationship was doomed, but I was hanging on because I didn't want to hurt my ex-boyfriend. Eventually, we decided to call it quits. After a few months, Carson tracked me down and admitted his feelings...and here we are."

"Uh-huh. Did you have any thoughts or feelings for him before he confessed his undying love?"

The sarcasm in his voice is hard to miss. It makes me want to put him in his place, but he's mostly right. Carson *is* lying to him. I can't speak for the man who's capturing my heart, but I'll definitely defend myself because the truth works in my favor.

"Actually, I did. From the moment we met, he stuck in my memory. Of course, I would never have been unfaithful to my boyfriend while we were together, and I really had no way of knowing Carson felt about me the way I did about him. After my ex and I split, I didn't want to look like a fool and throw myself at Carson. But when he called me to say that he'd never forgotten me and wanted me to come to North Carolina to explore what might be between us... Well, I'd been unhappy in my love life, and I had wondered once or twice if he had something to do with it. I had nothing to lose by coming here. So I said yes."

"Right," he says skeptically. "Did he tell you that he's engaged?"

"He told me everything. And we both agreed that with his wedding to Kendra coming up, we couldn't afford to wait another minute to find out how we felt about each other or it would be too late."

"So you knew that I'd challenged him to introduce you to me before you ever stepped foot on the plane? And your decision to come here had everything to do with your heart and nothing to do with helping him bilk me out of millions of dollars?"

My decision to come here had everything to do with me needing rent money...and being curious about the guy I'd never managed to forget. Carson's rival didn't cross my mind at all, except to wonder why he expected to control his adult daughter.

"Mr. Shaw, you don't know me, so I'll let that insult slide. But don't suggest again that I'm the sort of mercenary woman who would take a job simply for the terrible motive of stealing someone's hard-earned fortune."

His mouth flattens into a grim line. "Then how do you explain the money he transferred into your bank account the day you left?"

I'm shocked. I didn't know Shaw even knew my name before I introduced myself. I didn't think he'd go so far as to invade my privacy and have me investigated. "Not that it's any of your business, but he agreed to pay for my plane ticket and a few other expenses I incurred for dropping everything and coming to visit him so quickly."

Which is basically true. I'm not being paid the fee we negotiated until the end of our agreement.

I don't think he expected me to have explanations for his pointed questions, because he studies me with a dissecting stare, like he's trying to discern the truth. "You have odd jobs and no money to your name because you're a wannabe actress. Why shouldn't I believe he staged some long-distance casting call, plucked you out of a crowd, and hired you?"

I try not to blanch, but he's asked the one question I don't have an answer for that isn't a blatant lie.

"Because I met her before I moved here and became engaged to Kendra, and I can prove it." Carson rescues me, wrapping his arm around my waist and flashing Shaw a picture on his phone.

I recognize it instantly. A snapshot of the night we met at Shane's party. I vaguely remember posing for this picture, the birthday boy hanging awkwardly off my left and Carson pressed against me on the right. Some more friends crowded around us, but I swore I could feel the heat of Carson's skin on mine for hours.

He must have had this on his phone all along, and I can't help but hope it's because he wanted to look at us together over the last few months, not because he was too lazy to delete it.

At Shaw's glare, Carson hits the screen and displays the date of the photo. Suddenly, March seems like a lifetime ago.

"So you knew each other before you moved here." Shaw shrugs Carson's way. "It doesn't mean you've ever had a thing for her."

"Your suspicion also doesn't mean that I haven't," Carson shoots back, nudging me behind his back and positioning himself between me and Shaw protectively. "If you have an accusation, say it to me. But you don't get to badger and insult her. That's a nonstarter."

His words warm me. Butterflies start dancing. Sure, his behavior might all be an act...but given what I know about this man and the way we've been getting close, I don't think so.

"Daddy?" Kendra appears just outside the confrontation, grabbing his arm. "This isn't good for the cause."

I look around and realize that some of the attendees are watching with interest, seeming to hang on our every word.

Shaw seems to realize it, too. He pastes on a sudden smile. "Perhaps you're right, and I'm utterly wrong."

He doesn't believe that for a moment, but that's fine—for now. The public confrontation is over. The reckoning will come later. Soon. In fact, it's possible he'll even find some way to maneuver a word with us in private before we leave the hotel this evening.

When he sticks out a hand, Carson pumps it furiously. "You are."

"Let's dance, Daddy." Kendra pulls on the man's arm.

With a curt nod, Shaw takes his daughter's hand and leads her onto the floor.

I breathe a sigh of relief.

Carson turns to me and cups my shoulders. "You all right?"

"Yeah. I handled him pretty well until you approached. The rest of his questions we'd planned for and I didn't have to outright lie," I whisper in his ear. "But the last one..."

"I know." He brushes a kiss over my lips. "We should dance, too. Look like we're having a good time. It's probably the best place to have an uninterrupted conversation."

"You're right." I follow him onto the floor and brush my body against his as he takes my hand, swaying to an Ellie Goulding tune that's both haunting and hopeful.

I nestle closer and take a moment to close my eyes. My argument with Shaw was stressful, but being near Carson calms me.

"What did he say to you before I crashed the conversation?"

I fill him in with a shrug. "The truth is, I don't think he's a terrible guy. I think he actually means well where Kendra is concerned. But he's going about everything the wrong way. Obviously, he's used to telling people to jump and them asking immediately, 'How high?' When I didn't follow suit, it frustrated him."

"That sounds about right. I don't think he means to be an asshole, either. He wants to take care of his daughter. After my last conversation with her, I completely understand why."

"Yeah?" I look up into Carson's blue eyes. I'll never get tired of the view. "What did she want?"

"I think I told you that before you arrived, I called Kendra to tell her that you were coming here so we could figure out our feelings for each other. We never talked much before that. Our engagement was arranged before we'd barely met. Apparently, she thought I was determined to make her my wife. Now that she knows otherwise, she's opened up about her own feelings. Tonight, she wanted to tell me about Brayden, the ROTC officer she met on Tuesday, and their 'ah-mazing' spontaneous date last night."

I raise a brow at Carson. "That doesn't sound good."

"Apparently someone has a video of them kissing...um, vigorously, in the parking lot. Everyone here probably already knew except me, since I've been too busy with you."

"So she wanted to tell you herself?"

He nods. "In all honesty, I don't care. I want her to be happy, of course. But I'm not sure she's mature enough to know what will make her life sunshine and rainbows. She has the body of a woman, but when it comes to men, she's like a child with a basket of toys, swapping one out for another on a whim. Brayden is probably just the latest. Though I will say, she sounds more interested in him as a person than she has the others I've overheard her mooning about."

"The others?" My jaw drops. "Has she been dating the whole time you've been engaged?"

"Dating might be a strong word. But flirting would be fair."

"Batting her lashes or actually getting to know them?"

"Probably both. I've never asked, and she's never confided. I wasn't even aware until recently that she'd lose her trust fund if she bailed on me."

"Do you think she's slept with other men?"

"That's something I've never asked. If I had to guess? Yeah. I didn't exactly discourage her from seeing her friends, going to parties, or any of the usual college antics."

I gape at him. It's terrible that neither he nor Kendra is devoted to each other in the slightest, but neither knows how to put the kibosh on their pending nuptials without losing everything they value.

"So she wanted to tell you about Brayden. Because she suddenly wanted your blessing? I don't understand."

"I think Kendra wants someone to confide in. She can't tell her father that she thinks this one might be serious."

"How can she believe that? She's only known him for a couple of days." Instantly, I realize what I've said. I press my lips to his ear. "I know that's technically true of us, too. But...I think we're different."

He brushes his thumb across my cheek with a smile. "I think so, too. I'll admit I've never heard Kendra as intent about a guy as she is about this one. Brayden doesn't sound like her usual frat-boy crush, so maybe this is more than a flirtation or a fling. Anyway, she said that after watching you and me together as we walked in, she realized that—" He stops abruptly, frowns, pauses, and seems to regather himself. "Well, she suggested we work together to make everyone mutually happy."

I frown. What did he *not* say? To dissuade her dad from forcing you two to get married?"

"That sums it up."

"Great. How did she suggest you two do that?"

"She didn't," he admits wryly. "She left it up to me to devise a plan."

"Naturally. Do you trust her?"

"In a relationship?" He shakes his head. "But we have a common goal here, so in this case I believe she's on our side."

Carson knows Kendra better than I do, so I'll go with him on this. But I still have to ask one question. "You didn't tell her anything about...us?"

"Not a word. She's not the malicious sort who would rat us out, but she's not cautious enough to stay silent."

I agree. "So now what?"

"We wait. We eat, drink, laugh, kiss, schmooze. And at the end of the night, I'll confront Shaw."

CHAPTER SIX

CARSON

The next three hours pass in agony. I feel Shaw's eyes on us every moment of this gala. He's across the table from Ella and me during dinner. He's beside me as we each wait for our turn to speak at the center stage podium about this great cause. He's following us as we head to the bar for another drink, work the room, dance some more... Finally, I glance at my watch. It's nearly midnight, and my prospective father-in-law is still giving us the critical stare.

When Ed Sheeran sounds over the speakers, I grab Ella's hand. If the evening is going to end in disaster with Shaw refusing to believe that I have feelings for her, I don't know what I'll do next. If I sacrifice Sweet Darlin', I'll put over a thousand employees at five different plants out of work. I'll fail in a task I studied to accomplish my entire academic career. I'll end my late father's dream.

But goddamn it, I want Ella. I want to be with her more than I thought possible. We could have something real and strong and lasting if we simply had better circumstances.

Since we don't, I don't know where that leaves us.

"Hey," Ella murmurs softly, her fingertips caressing the back of my neck, drifting over my shoulders. "Are you all right?"

"Maybe." I shake my head solemnly. "I don't think Shaw is going to budge on the idea of marrying me off to his daughter for a stake of Sweet Darlin', and I'm going round and round in my head."

"About what to do next?"

I nod. "Kendra and I don't belong together, and I'd like to spare us both the heartache. But I also know what my mom and stepdad would have said about the fact I've been lying to a man to whom I gave my word. I hate not doing the honorable thing." I sigh. As long as I'm putting my cards on the table, I might as well show Ella the ones I tucked up my sleeve. "And now I'm worried about something else." I cup her cheek. "I don't want to lose you."

Her face softens. "I don't want to lose you, either. To be honest, I didn't expect all the feelings..."

"Me, either." I press my lips together in what I know must be a grim line. Everything about this moment feels sadly inevitable. "I'm having these crazy thoughts..."

Her brow furrows in concern. "Like what?"

"If we tried to make this work for real, in the long run, how would we manage it so we could both be happy? Am I the only one thinking that way?"

"No," she whispers, to my relief. "Scenarios have crossed my mind, too. But I don't have any answers."

"Yeah." I shake my head in agreement. "No matter what we do, someone has to give up something big."

"We're not in an easy position, are we?"

We turn quiet, and I'm sure we both wish everything could be as simple as the last couple of days have been. Breathing with Ella is effortless. So is sleeping, laughing, talking, cuddling, eating...just being together.

Why is everything suddenly so fucking complicated?

As the song ends, I pull her close. I hate this feeling of being torn in multiple directions and having no control over my life. I want to damn Shaw. I even want to damn myself for being desperate enough to take his deal. But none of that changes where we are and the fact that I may have to make some difficult decisions after tonight. My earlier decision to put space between Ella and me seems more logical...but less possible. I'd far rather tell her how I feel and simply let the chips fall. We might not end up together, but at least I'll know I was one hundred percent honest with her.

"Let's not worry right now," she whispers, then she leans in to kiss me.

Avoidance of the problem, I know. But as I meet her halfway and press my lips to hers, that sounds damn fine.

The moment we kiss, the room seems to fade away. The music disappears. I'm left with only the sound of my beating heart and the feel of her clinging to my shoulders.

In that moment, I want to give her my breath, my future, and my heart.

I pull back, smooth a dark curl from her face, and swallow hard. "I think I'm in love with you."

Her face is blank for a terrible moment. Then excitement dances in her eyes. Her lips curl up in a joyous smile. Happiness brightens her whole face. I find myself smiling back.

Ella blushes, bites her lip. "I think I'm in love with you, too."

She sobers for a moment, seeming to remember, as I do, that

our feelings don't change our circumstances. Someone is going to have to give up something in order for us to be together. Or we'll have to part ways. There's no way to have our cake and eat it, too.

"Oh, how touching," Gregory Shaw drawls as he dances Kendra across the floor in the opposite direction.

Kendra sends me a pleading stare of apology. She's trying... within the scope of what she can do. Her father doesn't listen to her—or to anyone.

"It is, actually," I snarl because I've had enough of him manipulating me. "Stop spitting out the most sarcastic quip in every scenario and start caring more about the fact that you're making everyone around you—even your own daughter—unhappy for the sake of some ambition or rivalry none of us even understands." I stop dancing and grab Ella's hand. "You know my heart is with Ella. But if you want to keep pushing and force me to marry Kendra, you'll wind up with a disaster. I'll bury myself in work to make sure you never gain another smidgen of influence at Sweet Darlin'. Don't expect grandchildren. And don't be surprised when your daughter sneaks around behind my back and breaks her marriage vows repeatedly. I won't stop her because I know she'll be looking for a deep, true love—something we don't share. She'll come to resent you for her loneliness and the impossible position you've put her in. She'll run off the second she comes into her trust fund. There won't be a damn thing either of us can do to stop her. So unless you want to see us in divorce court in three years, I suggest you find another tactic. Or go fuck yourself." I tug on Ella's hand. "Let's go."

She follows me off the floor, squeezing my hand tightly in silent support. I don't know who overheard us and I don't care anymore.

If I have to marry Kendra in fifteen days, it doesn't matter if people know neither of us is happy before the vows. I'm sure it will be obvious as hell to them afterward.

As I open the door for Ella, I'm so glad to escape the hotel. I give the valet my claim check. He dashes off and we wait to make our final escape.

"That was a good speech," she praises me.

"It was the truth. I hope I didn't just fuck everything up."

"What you said needed to be said. If Shaw doesn't see how right you are, it's because he doesn't want to."

I nod. "But it also doesn't change anything, sweetheart. I either have to break the deal altogether and come to you a poor man with nothing that resembles the means to make a productive livelihood or ask you to wait for Kendra to come into her trust fund when she's twenty-five and I've managed to divorce her. That's three years from now."

She must feel my tension because she fits herself against me, buffering me from the lash of hot wind and anger with a hug, cupping my cheek in her hand. "We don't have to have all the answers tonight."

"No, but if we're going to last, we need them soon."

Ella doesn't argue. She knows I'm right.

"I'm sorry," I say into the silence.

"For what?"

"Dragging you into this hopeless situation. If I'd had any inkling we'd wind up here…"

"In love and unable to see a way we can be together?" She caresses my face. "How could you have known?"

"I called you, rather than someone else, because you made me feel something when we met."

"And besides the money, I said yes for the same reason." She gives me a sad smile. "Even if we can't stay together, I wouldn't have missed spending this time with you for anything. I've looked for love for years without knowing what I want or need out of a relationship. Now, I do. I'll probably never find it again," she admits softly. "But at least I'll know."

Damn it, how is this woman so amazing?

The car arrives, and the valet helps Ella inside. We share a silent ride home, me steering with one hand and curling my fingers around hers with the other. All I can think about is being close to her.

The trip seems like the longest fifteen minutes of my life, but we're finally pulling up in front of my building. Without exchanging a word, we make our way through my door. The mood has a solemn excitement that confuses me. We both know our time may be limited to a number of days we can count with fingers and toes. But we're together now, alone, aware that we're falling for each other.

She sets her purse on the hall table just inside the door. I toss my car keys beside it. Our stares meet. The pull between us tugs and pings. Our chemistry takes up all the air in the room.

"Show me the zipper on your dress."

Ella turns her back to me, lifting her hands to unwind her hair from its elegant updo. As I pinch the tab and tug, parting the silk, her hair comes tumbling down, the long curls brushing the pale skin halfway down her back. I caress her shoulders, draping the delicate straps of her dress over her arms. The fabric is so silky it clings to her every curve as it slinks to the floor. Before I even speak, she steps out of the silken puddle, clad only in a strapless bra, a sexy-as-hell thong, and heels that make her legs look endless and lean.

"Take off your panties," I murmur in her ear, gratified when she shudders and complies. I unclasp her bra at the same time. They both litter the floor moments later, just beside her shimmering dress. But she's still not naked, and I need her to be. "Shoes."

At my prompt, Ella steps out of them and onto the hardwood floor. She slides closer, until her backside cradles my front. She's bare from head to toe, her soft skin abrading the fabric of my tux as I splay a palm over her abdomen and caress my way up to cradle her heavy breast. When I bend to kiss her neck, she tilts her head to give me more access to her graceful throat and lets loose a groan. I nip and suck at her while my other hand finds its way between her legs, fingers sinking between her folds. She's completely drenched.

"Why so wet?" I ask as I toy with her clit. "What have you been thinking about, sweetheart?"

She doesn't play coy. "You. What would happen as soon as we came through the door. How good it would feel."

I arch my hips, nudging her ass with my hard cock. "I've been thinking the same thing. I want you now, Ella."

She pants, her head falling back against me. Her eyes close as she writhes under my touch. God, she's so beautiful without knowing it, so sensual without being aware of her own feminine power.

"Yes."

"Do you want to come on my fingers or with me buried inside you?" I nip at her lobe, smiling slightly as she trembles in my arms.

"I have to choose?"

"Don't be greedy," I scold, suppressing a laugh. "Tell me how you want to come."

"With you inside me," she gasps out.

Her answer thrills me. I'd like that, too. I won't deny I'd like to simply watch her in the throes of ecstasy for the sheer visual enjoyment, but I'm not sure my patience will allow that.

Regretfully, I step away and release Ella, holding out my hand to her. "Come with me."

She sets her palm on mine without hesitation. Our eyes meet. The thread of connection between us thickens, strengthens. It's a completely new experience, yet I have no doubt that's what this feeling is.

With an absent flip of the lock on the door, I lead her through the bedroom and into the bathroom. I have a giant soaking tub I've never used. And suddenly I want to inaugurate it the right way.

In the middle of the room, I grip her hips. "Stop."

Ella does without hesitation, and my head swims with all the possible demands I could make of her body. She would undoubtedly surrender to them, to me. That notion is heady. I've always liked to be in control in bed, but with her the need has ratcheted up to a whole new level.

I turn her to face me. Our eyes meet. The moment is a profound thrill. The gravity of connecting the first time we've acknowledged our feelings mixes with pure sexual hunger to concoct a dizzying desire I doubt will end with our orgasms.

"Up you go, sweetheart." I lift her onto the counter.

She settles herself on the marble and spreads her legs to me in invitation. I'm never going to turn that down.

"Wait here." I press a kiss onto her forehead. I don't dare take her mouth now. If I do, I won't let her go until we've both found climax.

"Hurry," she breathes as she leans back onto the bathroom mirror, skimming her fingertips along the insides of her splayed thighs.

Yeah, with a visual like that, you bet I will.

I brush my hand over her knee as I make my way out of the bathroom, tearing through the bedroom, and into the home office down the hall. I pick up the rolling stool, then approach my bed again, stopping at the nightstand to retrieve a foil packet from the box inside.

When I return to the bathroom, Ella sends me a questioning stare. "I understand what the condom is for, but the stool?"

I don't reply, merely smile as I set the rolling contraption in the middle of the room, start the tub, then adjust the tap until the water is the right temperature. Once it is, I plug up the drain, leaving the water trickling in the background.

Then I lower myself onto the padded stool and roll my way between Ella's delicious thighs. Without preamble, I grip her knees in my hands, dangle her calves down my back, and fasten my mouth over her pussy. Her flavor is an addiction. So are her responses—immediate and without filter. She loves being worshipped, and I'm more than happy to make her feel like a goddess.

Within moments, she threads her fingers through my hair and tries to pull me deeper. She gasps, groans, whimpers, the sounds a beautiful symphony of pleasure filling my ears.

"Carson?" She sounds almost panicked.

Yes, she feels me. She wants this. She's only moments away. Granted, this isn't the mutual orgasm we discussed earlier...but I don't hear her complaining.

To help her find satisfaction now, I plunge a pair of fingers into her, relishing the feel of her flesh clinging to my digits because she's yearning to be filled, desperate for the friction. I find the smooth skin along her front wall and rub slowly, methodically, unrelentingly.

Within seconds, she's scratching at me, begging with her grasping hands and unintelligible pleas. Her clit swells on my tongue. Her pussy grips my fingers mercilessly. I moan against her flesh.

She explodes.

Her back arches as she growls out a climax like I've never heard from her—deep, wrenching, and endless. The sounds mimic the crescendo of pleasure that builds inside her, rising to a loud cacophony of cries that echo off the walls.

I hold in a smile as I lap and suck and stimulate her until her entire body goes limp.

"You're insatiable," she manages to say weakly, but she's wearing a loopy little grin that tells me she's not at all unhappy about that fact.

"You're welcome," I quip as I roll across the floor to kill the tap to the tub.

The water level looks perfect, and gentle tendrils of steam rise up invitingly.

She eyes the tub. "Are we cleaning up already?"

"No, sweetheart. I'm definitely going to dirty you up some more."

"If that's the case, you're overdressed."

My tux is wrinkled, and my shirt feels limp after a full night of festivities and a few minutes in the humid bathroom. I'm ready to ditch it all.

"You're right." I stand and tug at my bow tie, then shed my shoes, jacket, pants, and once stiffly starched shirt... Finally, I stand before her, every bit as naked as she is, then I help her off the counter and into my arms.

With a hand in her soft, dark tresses, I guide her mouth to mine and feast on her tongue, going deep, letting her taste herself and feel my passion that's been simmering and stewing while I sent her into a spinning climax. She clings to me, not quite steady on her feet as she gives me every part of herself, settling her breasts on my chest, gripping my neck, caressing the side of my leg with her calf.

She's perfect against me and about to take me deep into her body. I've never felt a certainty that a woman is meant to be meaningful to me. Sure, I might have wanted another date—or a second dance of the mattress tango—to test the chemistry. But this need isn't stemming from my libido.

Reluctantly, I release her and step into the tub I've intentionally only half filled. As the warm water encloses my feet and the lower part of my legs, I help her in, too, wrapping my arms around her to dust kisses along the graceful slope of her shoulder. Everything about this woman fascinates me.

"It's a big tub, but I don't think we're both going to get clean in here," she teases.

"Totally not the point." I don't give her time to ask questions before I sit in the shimmering water, bracing myself against the sloped back and donning my condom as she watches with an unblinking stare as water laps around my hips. "Straddle me."

The light bulb illuminates in her head, and her entire face

brightens as she positions her feet on either side of my thighs and sinks to her knees. I hold my cock by the base, pointing straight up at her as she settles the crest at her opening and begins to sink down with a sigh of pleasure.

"I've wanted to do this," she admits.

"Make love in a bathtub?"

Ella shakes her head. "No, but I like that, too. What I've really wanted is to be on top. You're always so in control of me during sex. I wanted to, um...return the favor."

As she sinks down to the hilt, her breath becomes a long moan. I hiss between my teeth at the bliss of having her wrapped around me, her flesh swollen after her recent peak, yet eager for more. I take her by the hips and guide her back up my aching cock.

I need her. And I need her now.

"Not so fast." She stops me, grinding down on my length. "It's my turn."

I think of all the times I've teased and tormented her, dragging out her pleasure, denying her orgasm, holding her just outside the reach of the sensation that would send her toppling into the abyss of satisfaction. I'm sure if she has the chance, she'll repay me.

The water sloshes as she rises up, then sinks back down, one protracted inch at a time, awakening every one of my nerve endings to the feel of her encasing me and the ecstasy to come. Yeah, she's going to undo me thoroughly, and I'm okay with that—eventually.

But I'm not going down easily or alone.

I tug on her shoulders and send her toppling against me before cradling a breast and lifting it to my mouth. "Then ride me."

She does as I torment her nipples, gently sucking, nipping,

gnawing until I know she's feeling me. Her skin turns rosy again. Her pussy tightens. Her pace quickens.

"Carson..." Her protest is almost a mewl. She wriggles like the ache is growing too much too fast.

"Sweetheart?" When she doesn't say anything for a long moment, I wonder if it's because she can't string her thoughts together...or if she's plotting something. "Let me help you."

"No." She shakes her head as she thrusts down on me again, this time a bit faster. Water splashes around us, the displacement growing with every movement. "No."

Since she's panting her denial, I grip her hips. "But I insist."

Then I bend my knees, brace my feet on the bottom of the tub, and shove my way up inside her, owning her tight depths, plunging deeper than I've ever been. My cock nudges the spot along her inner wall that I worked with my fingers. It should be hypersensitive now.

"Oh, my god." Her eyes flash wide and she looks at me, mouth gaping in astonishment. "Yes!"

Ella wails out her assent as she grabs my shoulders, fingernails digging into my skin, forearms braced on my chest.

I repeat the motion, fucking her thoroughly from beneath. In the next thrust, she joins the rhythm. Her whole body falls into it— head tossed back, hips flowing with me. After another roll through the water together, we're in sync and scaling our way to mutual satisfaction. I don't care about the water spilling onto the tile floor. I don't care that my neighbors might be hearing the loud, high-pitched sounds of her need pinging throughout the room. I only give a damn about her and giving her the most pleasure possible. I can't deepen our commitment when I'm technically engaged to someone else, but I can drench her in orgasmic bliss. I can use my body as an expression of my devotion.

We move with common purpose wordlessly, linked by our need. I imagine an alternate universe where I'm free of Gregory Shaw and my obligation to marry Kendra. Where I've slid a ring on Ella's finger and we've spoken sweet, solemn vows. I've come home from work, and she's spent the day doing whatever makes her happy and contributes to her dream coming true. We're settled and ready for the future, and I'm not wearing this damn strangling condom because we're eager to start the next generation, fueled by the love and passion filling us now.

That, and her breasts bouncing near my mouth, is all it takes for me to zoom up to the zenith of pleasure. I manage to catch her nipple between my lips and suckle it until she's hissing and crying out and clamping down, heading for completion. As the feeling picks up steam, I fight through a haze of desire to keep plying her with sensation.

This is going to fucking ruin me.

"I'm close," I growl.

"Me, too," she keens out. "I'm there. I..." Her strangled scream of satisfaction swallows the rest.

I bury my face against her skin as the need converges into a thick knot of desperate ache. When I slam up inside Ella with the next thrust, it unravels. I lose all control. We collide again as the rapture takes over. I empty my body, soul, and heart into this woman in a way I never have. I suspect I never will again.

I'm still panting and holding her close when that realization smacks me witless, along with the dawning recognition that I'm in love for the first—and last—time in my life.

I have no idea what to do next.

"Wow," she manages to murmur weakly as she pushes the hair away from her face.

"Wow." I'm still winded and sweating and bowled over.

She looks over the edge of the tub. "The floor is soaked. I'll get some towels."

When she makes to disconnect our bodies and rise, I hold her fast against me. "Just a minute."

Ella settles against me and meets my gaze, gnawing on her bottom lip. "Everything's changed, hasn't it?"

"Yes." I sigh. "And yet nothing has."

"I love you." She kisses me softly, with an air of mourning.

She knows we're on a countdown to goodbye unless something drastic changes or one of us gives up everything we hold dear.

Still, logic doesn't stop me from telling her exactly how I feel. "I love you, too."

"I wish I knew how to fix our mess," she says almost absently, knowing neither of us can, yet believing deep down there must be a solution because the world can't be that unfair.

I'm already sure it can be.

"Me, too, sweetheart. We have about two weeks to figure it out. Maybe it's time for a really honest conversation about what we both can live with...and can't live without."

Ella wriggles free and rises from the tub in another splash, gleaming beautifully in the warm overhead light. "We have and it still looks hopeless."

Wrapping a towel around herself, she avoids looking at me.

Tears well in her eyes. I want to hold her more than anything. I want to be a part of the solution.

But I already know I'm the problem. I've created this. Somehow, I'll have to fix it.

CHAPTER SEVEN

ELLA

Saturday dawns lazily. Carson and I spent the night in each other's arms, talking, kissing, making love. I don't think we ever slept, merely dozed for short stretches until the need to be close woke us again.

With a sleepy smile, I stretch, languid bliss filling every muscle from the tips of my fingers to the bottoms of my toes. Beside me, Carson snores lightly. Sunlight streams through his bedroom window, the sun appearing high in the sky. I glance at the clock and blink. How is it almost noon?

After a quick brush of my teeth and a shower, I step out of the stall, dripping and surprisingly refreshed—if sore—when I hear a pounding on the door. I stick my head out of the bathroom to see Carson rising, disoriented, and reaching for his robe with a scowl.

"Are you expecting anyone?"

He shakes his head as he belts his robe around his middle. "I usually get some quiet work done on weekends while vegging on my sofa. No one ever interrupts my weekends."

I shrug. I don't have any idea who could possibly be demanding admittance.

With a curse, he exits the bedroom. "Wait here."

After he shuts the door behind him, I hurry into a pair of shorts and a tank top. Summer in the South is no joke. Today promises to be another scorcher. I toss my hair into a ponytail, then creep across the bedroom, pressing my ear to the door, hoping to hear what's going on in the living room. I can make out two men's garbled voices.

Carson might have told me to wait, but I'm desperately curious. And I need coffee.

When I crack open the door, I see him pouring himself a mug, and Gregory Shaw, of all people, is watching him from a stool at the breakfast bar, sipping on his own cup of brew. When I step into the room, they both turn at the sound of my entrance.

"Morning," I murmur, trying to keep the surprise out of my voice.

"Good morning," Shaw returns smoothly.

When the other man isn't looking, Carson gives me a subtle little shrug. So he doesn't know what's going on or why his nemesis has invaded his home turf yet. A little knot of worry starts forming in the pit of my stomach.

The silence in the room grows awkward. No one speaks. Carson and I remain quiet because we're confused. I can only guess what's running through Shaw's head.

"The benefit last night went well. It looked as if the charity will receive a nice payday," I venture.

Shaw nods with a polite smile. "We won't have all the details about the final totals until tomorrow, but I suspect this year's donations will exceed last year's. The charity does important work, and I'm glad to be a part of it."

"As am I," Carson points out. "It's a cause I believe in."

"It looks fantastic," I add to keep the conversation rolling.

"With this year's funds, they're hoping to begin some after-school programs for kids and teenagers to keep them safe and off the streets," Shaw says.

"Then I'll hope this year's tally is really fat. Living in Los Angeles, I see a lot on the evening news about what happens in rough neighborhoods when gangs and drugs take over."

"It's happening everywhere." Shaw looks at Carson, hooking his thumb in my direction. "This one has a soft heart."

"She does, and I wouldn't want her any other way."

I hear the subtle warning in Carson's tone. Shaw didn't threaten me, merely made an observation. But one reason I love Carson is his protective side. He takes care of me in ways little and big. After having virtually no one to rely on for most of my life, it's a lovely luxury. I can handle myself—while taking care of my younger sisters, too. But I love the way Carson watches over me.

I cross the kitchen. As I do, he pours me a cup of coffee. With a kiss on my cheek, he hands it over before wrapping his arm around me. I nestle against his body. I don't like Shaw being here. It feels like an invasion. But being this close to Carson makes me feel safer.

He leans against the counter, keeping me pressed against him. "What brings you here this morning?"

Shaw chuckles. "Technically, it's afternoon. I've been up since six."

"After a late night, we slept in." Carson gives him a tight smile.

I refrain from elbowing him in the stomach. Maybe that statement could be taken several ways, but since he's wearing his bathrobe and still has bedhead, I doubt Shaw misunderstood Carson's meaning. Why announce to your prospective father-in-law that you spent all night in bed with another woman? Is he making a point—again—that he isn't attached to Kendra? I'm not convinced another reminder will help Shaw get the concept. He knows. He just doesn't care.

"As it happens, so has Kendra. I was concerned when she didn't come home last night. I texted and called... Of course I know she's a grown woman, but she didn't mention that she had plans to...go out. But she's fine."

"Brayden?" Carson asks.

Shaw clears his throat. "That's my understanding. She came home about seven this morning looking very...happy. Hours of worry followed by her glowing smile gave me some perspective. Oh, and your very insightful speech at the benefit last night." He pauses, his smile almost self-deprecating.

I don't trust it.

"And?" Carson prompts.

"It will take me a moment to explain. If you'll bear with me..." He turns his attention on me. "You love Frost?"

Carson and I exchange a glance. It's not as if we haven't been saying the words to one another all night, but we also haven't voluntarily shared our feelings with anyone else. They're new. They're precious. I know I need to call my sisters and tell them how deeply I've fallen. But for right now, what's in our hearts has just been for us, despite what Shaw overheard.

Still, I'm not going to lie. "Yes."

Shaw flips his gaze over to Carson. "And you—"

"Yes, I love her, and she knows it. I assume this question has a point?"

"Well, love is in the air, it seems. Kendra tells me she thinks she's in love, as well."

I hear the sarcastic drawl in his voice. He doesn't believe his daughter's feelings are true. I'm not sure he believes what Carson and I have is real, either.

"Well, if she is, I applaud her. I think everyone deserves to find someone who makes them happy and completes them." I say the words almost defiantly, as if willing Shaw to admit that he doesn't believe in love or care about his daughter's heart.

"*If* she is, perhaps. But one has to be practical, as well."

Beside me, Carson tenses. I grip his hand at my waist. Is Shaw really going to give us a speech that love is all good and fine, but money and power are more important?

"I don't think any amount of money is worth a lifetime of misery, Mr. Shaw. If you had to choose between your fortune and having your late wife back, which would you pick? Have you been happy without her?"

Shaw cocks his head and stares at me with a considering glance before he addresses Carson again. "Beautiful, a big heart, and a smart cookie, too. She's the real deal."

But I notice he didn't actually answer the question.

"Say what you came to say." Carson sounds curt, on edge.

"Less than ten minutes, and I'm already wearing out my welcome." Shaw chuckles to himself. "All right. After your speech last night and my daughter's pleas this morning, I came to change the terms of our arrangement. Far be it from me to keep a pair of lovebirds apart, so if you and Ms. Hope truly want to be together, you can have the venue, catering, flowers, cake—everything I've paid for when you and Kendra intended to tie the knot. I'll give it to you and Ella for free. All you have to do is say 'I do' on the day you'd already planned to marry. Then we'll continue our arrangement as normal. I'll give you the loan for Sweet Darlin'. You'll give me a five percent interest until the loan is repaid. And that will be the end of our connection."

I bite my lip to keep my gasp in. Get married? We haven't even figured out how to be together beyond my visit here. We haven't worked out any of the specifics about how we'd spend our lives together. Our relationship is still so new. So are our problems.

Carson's grip tightens on me protectively. "And if we don't get married?"

"Well, you always have door number one. You can marry Kendra, as planned. Or..." He smiles as if he's just been waiting to deliver these words. "You can sign over a ten percent interest—and ten percent of the profits—of Sweet Darlin' and you'll never have to repay me."

I'm shocked. I'm horrified, too. I suspect, given enough time and the right circumstances, Carson and I might naturally want to get hitched. But to have this man coerce us into it within the next two weeks or threaten to take more of the beloved business Carson inherited is outrageous.

I glare at Shaw. "Listen to me, you—"

"No," Carson says flatly. "Ella's life—and heart—aren't for bargaining."

"So you'd rather marry Kendra? Because I can, with a few

choice words, make that happen."

"You're her father," I say in horror. "Why would you force unhappiness on her?"

"Precisely because I am her father," he bites back. "If I don't guide her, Kendra will wind up without a career and without a guiding hand to steer her life. She'll blow through her trust fund in five years and spend the rest of her life penniless and alone after I'm gone. I'd like to prevent that from happening."

He might have a point about Kendra's behavior, but I don't agree with his methods. "If you're this concerned about your daughter, why push Carson and me to get married? How does that help her?"

"It doesn't. He's calling our bluff," Carson murmurs in my ear. "He still thinks we're putting on an act so I don't have to marry Kendra. He's making us put up or shut up."

Is the guy dense? "But you overheard us admit our love for each other on the dance floor last night."

As soon as the words are out of my mouth, I realize he's merely cynical.

"All for show," he replies. "I don't ever like being outmaneuvered, but even less by someone I should be able to plot circles around. So I'm giving you the opportunity to make a decision. Honor the agreement you already made, accept my magnanimous gesture of a free wedding for you and Ms. Hope, or marry no one and forfeit an extra five percent as penance."

Somehow, Gregory Shaw has found a scenario in which he wins no matter what Carson picks. Unbelievable...

"And what happens to Kendra?" Carson asks. "If Ella and I get married in two weeks, how will you keep your daughter from all the terrible consequences you mentioned earlier?"

"That's an insightful question. Her beau of the moment, Brayden, seems like the first solid man she's ever voluntarily dated. He comes from a poor family and his father suffers from chronic medical issues, and they lack the money to pay the bills. Quite sad..."

I doubt very much that Shaw actually cares. He sees the man's condition as leverage against Kendra's latest flame, nothing more.

"You'll only be buying her a husband for three years," Carson points out.

Shaw shrugs. "I've done my digging. Brayden's a smart, cautious man. He'll temper Kendra. That's all I care about. A lot can happen in three years. They might even become deeply attached..."

I stare at the man, still stunned. He's not only comfortable in the puppet-master role, he relishes it. I don't see an ounce of moral discomfort anywhere in his expression. He genuinely believes he's justified and that he knows better than the rest of us. In fact, I bet that if I baited and shoved a bit, he would commend himself for improving Kendra's—and Carson's—situations.

And I'm unimportant. Expendable. The means to an end. No matter what Carson and I elect to do, Shaw either gets a solid son-in-law or more money. He comes out ahead.

I want to rail and hate him. Mostly, I just shake my head at his misguided manipulation.

"Get out," Carson insists, stepping forward. "I think you've said enough. I want you gone and—"

"Yes, I've obviously overstayed my welcome." Shaw pours the rest of his coffee down the drain and sets the mug on the counter. "There are a few caveats, of course. If you marry Ms. Hope, you must cohabitate and stay married for a minimum of ten years or I'll take immediate possession of that additional five percent of Sweet Darlin'. You can't be unfaithful—either of you—for that same period of time. Don't think I won't be watching." He cocks his head. "That covers everything, I believe. You have until noon tomorrow to decide."

CARSON

The moment Gregory Shaw shuts the door behind him, I look over at Ella. She's shell-shocked. The silence is so complete, the absence of sound is almost a buzzing in my ears. I don't know what to say. After the corner that bastard just put me in, I'm angry. I'm furious on her behalf, too. I even feel sorry for Kendra. She probably does need a guiding hand, but she doesn't need her father forcing one on her. She needs time to mature and some real-world experience. Maybe she even needs a good failure or two in her life. I doubt she's ever had one. Her father wouldn't allow it. Maybe he should.

But Kendra isn't my problem now. I need to focus on Ella, on what we do next. I need to say the right thing. What is that?

"I'm sorry." I wrap my arms around her.

To my relief, she hugs me back. Somewhere in the back of my head, I worried she would resent that I've inadvertently dragged her into this fucked-up mess.

"It's not your fault and not your doing. I hate the position he's put you in."

"Me, too."

Ella sips her coffee. "Hungry?"

After a night of sex, I was. But following a visit from Gregory

Shaw... "Not so much."

"You need to eat. Let me make you something. While I do, we'll talk. Maybe there's a scenario we haven't explored yet that won't leave anyone in a bind."

I nod, but I don't think it's possible. Shaw isn't stupid. He's thought of all the angles. I feel perpetually one step behind the asshole, and I need to catch up. He's been manipulating me toward the outcome he wants. I have to figure out how to maneuver him to my conclusion instead.

"Thanks." I sit on a barstool and watch Ella make herself at home in my kitchen.

I'm usually more of a loner, but I'm glad she's here. When I first made the agreement with Shaw to marry Kendra, I stewed in bottled-up silence because I was in the untenable position of having to wed a stranger or lose my father's legacy. This time, I'm not swimming in the cesspool of crap alone.

She rummages through the refrigerator. "Spinach and mushroom omelets okay?"

Nothing sounds terribly appealing at the moment... "Sure. That sounds great."

"Liar." Ella laughs. "You don't have to coddle my feelings, Carson. Just tell me how you see this situation with Shaw unfolding next. You can choke down the omelet if you need."

"Choke?" I frown.

"I said I would cook. I didn't say it would be gourmet."

Even when everything is shitty, this woman still makes me laugh.

But my temporary mirth runs out. I sigh. "I can't marry Kendra.

Really. It would ruin both our lives. I know Shaw doesn't see that. But she would come to resent me, and I have no doubt I'd feel trapped and angry and, over time, bitter. Even if we split up in three years when she got her trust fund, I..." I shake my head. "I don't want to be without you. I wouldn't ask you to wait for me. It's not fair."

As Ella whisks the eggs in a mixing bowl, I see her expression. That's her thinking face. Lips slightly parted, tongue just touching her bottom lip, a little frown furrowing between her brows. "Well, nothing about this is fair, so let's remove that word from this conversation."

Her observation makes me chuckle again. "You're right."

"As it happens, I think marrying Kendra is your worst option. It's the choice in which no one is happy except Gregory Shaw. I mean, I don't know your—I hesitate to use this word—fiancée very well..."

"Ex. I'll make that official ASAP," I assure her. I have to.

"I think that's a wise choice. I'm sure it will give both of you some relief. You wouldn't have hired me in the first place if you'd been even slightly excited about making her your wife."

It's true. "So that leaves me trying to choose between the two least shitty options in a steaming pile of poo."

"And they both smell to high heaven." She sends me an empathetic glance.

"Exactly. If I give that bastard ten percent of my company, I'll never be rid of him. He'll keep trying to exert his influence and stick his nose where it doesn't belong. He knows most of my executives and plant managers. He'll try to persuade them that, as a partial owner, he has rights and he should be involved at every level of the organization. With only five percent, most of them will laugh him off. But at ten?" I wince. "It's not a controlling interest, but it's a more effective argument since no one but a Frost has ever owned a smidgen of Sweet Darlin'. I can also buy his five percent back if we stick to the original terms of the loan. And honestly, the last thing I can afford to do is give Shaw a glimpse of my recipes or plans for the future."

"You're right. Can anyone else help you financially?"

"I've had several offers to buy the company, but they were all crazy lowballs. If I took one, I'd feel as if I were cashing out because it was easy. I don't want easy. I want amazing. I want rewarding. I want to control my own destiny. That means helming the company that's mine, not to mention choosing my own wife."

"That's understandable. And I don't want you to dishonor your biological father's memory. The connection you're forming with him, even posthumously, is important to you, I can tell. You shouldn't have to give up something that's become meaningful. So that leaves one option." She bites her lip. "I don't know where you're at emotionally, Carson, but I have to be honest. I'm not ready to commit to getting married. Besides all the reasons we've already identified, I..." She shrugs and tosses her hands in the air. "I think a couple should know each other more than four days before they decide to exchange forever vows."

She's absolutely right. My mother and Edward Frost are a great example of what happens when you marry someone you're passionate about but don't know well enough to determine if you're truly compatible. I'd rather not wind up divorced, especially if there are kids involved. I know firsthand that it sucks for everyone.

I rub my palms together—a nervous habit when I'm thinking. There must be some way out of this mess. I refuse to believe that Gregory Shaw has one-upped me and I'm going down.

"If we could have longer to get to know each other..." She pours the first batch of eggs into the pan. "If I could be sure my sisters would be all right without me in California... If there were some way for me to pursue my acting in North Carolina..."

I completely see her point. Everything she's said since Shaw left has been bouncing around in my brain. "You said something earlier about exploring all possibilities... What if our solution has no resemblance to any of the options that bastard gave us?"

"Go on." She sounds intrigued.

"You're an actress, and I can pretend fairly well, I think. He wants to call our bluff. What if we let him? What if we change up this poker match to play a game of chicken? First one to flinch loses."

"Why would he flinch?" Ella frowns.

"Deep down, he *wants* me to marry Kendra. After all, he doesn't know this Brayden dude. Okay, so his parents need money. But why would Shaw trust a stranger—and a poor one at that—with the multimillions Kendra will inherit when she comes into her trust fund? He knows I don't personally need her money and I'm not greedy, but Brayden..." I shrug. "He might be a great guy. But if he's not...well, in the South, they have a saying. And Shaw is too smart to let a fox into his henhouse."

"Yes." She smiles like she knows we're on to something, like she can feel it, too. "You're right."

"If Kendra marries Brayden, once the vows are spoken, Shaw will have virtually no leverage to control him. But if *I* marry her, he'll have his interest in Sweet Darlin' to ensure he maintains some power over me, at least for a few years until I've repaid him. The minute he truly believes I've walked away from Kendra and intend to marry you, he might be willing to negotiate."

"So you're suggesting we upgrade our pretending from girlfriend to fiancée?"

"Exactly."

Ella's face sobers before she turns to add veggies to the beaten eggs heating in the pan. "What happens when we don't go through with the wedding?"

"Not the right way to look at the situation. You should ask what happens if *you* don't go through with it. Before you came here, I told Shaw that I was exploring my feelings for you. I didn't know what yours were for me. I made that clear."

"Maybe so." Her cheeks turn slightly pink. "But he overheard my feelings on the dance floor at the benefit. We admitted them earlier this morning to his face."

"But I don't think that precludes us from using the rationale we crafted when we first planned our 'breakup.' Remember, your life is in LA and all that?"

"I do." When she turns to face me again, it's obvious she's catching on. "So instead of merely breaking up with you at the end of my visit, I'll simply jilt you at the altar. After all, you can't control me. And I have a suspicion about Gregory Shaw. He thinks his own daughter is flaky, so I'm pretty sure he would believe that's true of most women. Does he have any female executives?"

I do a mental scan of his staff. "Other than his assistant, no. All men, cronies who have been with him for decades."

"That's what I mean. It's possible he's a closet misogynist. So you can't help it if you were perfectly willing to proceed with the wedding but I backed out at the last minute and left you brokenhearted. I mean, it's not your fault if I'm flaky. I *am* one of those Hollywood types, after all. And I'm just a woman..."

Ella is incredibly down-to-earth. I can't think of anyone less stuck on herself or more likely to keep her promises. But Gregory Shaw won't take the time to get to know her. He should buy this.

"Of course," I drawl, glancing at Ella, who looks as if she wants to punch my rival in the face for his screwed-up attitude.

"The only problem is, he thinks our whole relationship is a ruse. We have to find some way to debunk that notion."

She's right. "What can we do that seems permanent to him during our 'engagement'?"

"I could fly home and drive my car back out." She wrinkles her nose, glancing over her shoulder to check the eggs. "But it's pretty crappy and I doubt it would make the long trip without dying altogether."

I shake my head. "That drive is too long for you to make alone, especially in an unreliable car. And I can't get away from work right now to travel with you. Every day in the office is critical until we get Sweet Darlin's balance sheet under control. What about...a job?"

"Like, actually accept a position to work here in North Carolina?"

"Exactly. And what I have in mind is up your alley, too. The children's charity is hoping to build those after-school programs, so they have an open position right now for an activities director. The role would put you in charge of kids' workshops. You can introduce them to the arts. You can help them learn music and stage plays..."

She raises her brows like she's actually interested, but then she scowls. "What makes you think they'd hire me?"

I send her a grin. "I know a guy who works there..."

"In other words, with you being such a big donor, they owe you a favor or two?"

"Something like that." It's sad she's not staying, because I honestly think she'd do great work there.

"It sounds like something I'd enjoy. But...I'd hate to hire on, then walk off the job abruptly. I'd be leaving them in a lurch."

I can't exactly refute her, but I'm a step ahead of her on a couple of salient points. "First, they're currently accepting résumés, so they'll still have a fresh stack of them when you—" I can't say leave. I don't want to think about Ella waving goodbye and getting on a plane forever. Somehow, we're going to find a solution to be together, damn it. "When you no longer need the job. At that point, they can slot in another qualified candidate. Hell, I'll even help them with a donation of holiday candy for their annual Santa Parade to ease the pain. Trust me, they'll be fine. Second, I don't want to screw anyone, either, but I love you and you love me...and getting Shaw off our backs could mean a lot for us."

Ella bobs her head as she reaches absently for the shredded cheese and tosses it into the omelet. As it melts, she does a little spatula magic, folds the concoction in half, and flips it over. "I just hate being dishonest. In fact, if you hadn't been the one to offer me this assignment, I might well have turned it down."

"I hate lying, too. But we can't afford to bring scruples to a gunfight."

"It sucks but it's true." She sighs, sprinkling a little more cheese on top of the omelet before sliding it onto a waiting plate and setting the steaming eggs in front of me.

"Thanks."

"You're welcome. Do you think me being gainfully employed in North Carolina will be enough to convince him that I intend to stay? He's a business owner, too. He must know people quit or abandon their jobs every day for all kinds of reasons."

"Good point." I smile absently as she hands me a fork and I dig into my breakfast. She also passes me a blueberry muffin I bought at the grocery store when I shopped the night before her arrival. I'm not surprised they haven't been touched. She's been watching every bite that crosses her lips since the indulgence from the steakhouse.

I take a bite out of both—and realize I'm hungrier than I thought. "I've got another idea. Something that should convince him we're serious is buying a house. I've been wanting to give up this cramped apartment and put down roots here. I haven't made the time to go house hunting. I really don't know what I'm looking for, other than something less temporary with more space."

"If we appeared to buy a house together..." She nods enthusiastically. "A job is easy to give up. A house isn't. If you're really okay with buying a place, I think that's a great idea."

"Let's do it. I'll make sure Shaw finds out when we pick the perfect one."

Suddenly, Ella laughs. "This tangled, twisted plot is making us pretend we're engaging in a lot of life-changing events all at once—starting a job, buying a house, getting married... It's crazy. You know that, right?"

"Batshit," I confirm with a nod. "But if anyone can manage it all, it's us."

She beams a smile at me. "Absolutely."

I reach across the breakfast bar and take her hand. "And Ella, we might be manipulating him, but we're right. Kendra and I don't belong together. I shouldn't have to give him years of my life or ten percent of my company. When you and I don't make it to the altar on Shaw's timetable, well...I'll hope that he's willing to fall back to standard business practices and simply lend me money in exchange for a small but temporary chunk of Sweet Darlin'. If he won't give me the money, I'll deal with it then."

"That's all you can do. So, if we're going to pretend to be engaged, what do we do first?"

"Let me call Kendra and give her the news. Then I'll contact her father and tell him that we intend to take that free wedding he offered. After that, we'll start playing the happy bride and groom. And we'll hope for the best in the end—for all of us."

As Ella whips up another omelet for herself, she gives me an absent nod, clearly still pondering the situation. I can't help but suspect she's thinking what I am: What happens to us after the ruse is over?

I don't have the answer to that question. I'm aware that our remaining time together probably isn't enough to make her want to give up everything she's built for herself in California and move here with me. But I have to try.

What other choice do I have that doesn't end in abject, miserable loneliness?

CHAPTER EIGHT

E L L A

After our discussion over breakfast, Carson and I both agreed we had tasks to accomplish if we intend to pull this ruse off successfully. He's stepped into his home office to call Kendra. They deserve the privacy of a quiet end to their ill-fated engagement. I clean the dishes, even though he told me he'd help me as soon as he made his fiancée his ex. It gives me something to do...other than call my younger sisters.

I hate lying to them, and I'll take a lot of crap for it later. But right now, I can't tell them I'm getting fake married. Eryn might be a mere two years younger than me, but she's about a billion years more cynical. I don't know if it's middle-child syndrome, her given personality, or the breakup she never recovered from. Either way, if I clue her in on what's happening, she'll tell me I'm crazy, that Carson is using me, and that the whole thing will only end badly. The baby of the family, Echo, is fun and bubbly and always has a smile. She's the sunshine to Eryn's rain cloud. I love her to pieces, but she can't keep a secret worth a damn.

I wouldn't go to the pretense of dragging them across the

country for a wedding that will never happen, except that Gregory Shaw knows my background. He knows I have sisters. He probably even knows we're close. I'll never convince the man I'm serious about getting married without them.

"Here goes nothing," I mutter to myself, plopping down on a barstool in the kitchen and dialing Eryn's number. She's far more likely to pick up since Echo misplaces her phone all the time.

"Hey!" she answers. "How's the hush-hush job you couldn't discuss? Got a southern accent yet?"

"Seriously? After four days, you think I've picked up a twang?"

"Maybe you should try harder to acquire one. It would be cute at your auditions. Besides, it would give me something to poke at you about. Because you're otherwise practically perfect."

"Hardly true. The job is..." *Good? Fine?* "Complicated."

Eryn pauses, her tone shifting to serious. "That doesn't sound good. Tell me what's up. You okay?"

I grope for something to say. I should have planned this speech a bit better, somehow eased her into it. Hindsight is awesome, but I've already stepped in it too deep to climb out now. "Is Echo there?"

"Right beside me, downing a bowl of Raisin Bran."

"I need to talk to you both. Put me on speaker so she can hear, too, okay?"

"Now you're really scaring me."

"It's actually a good thing." I try to sound convincing.

"Uh-huh," Eryn drawls. "Hold on." A moment passes, and the background has a slight hiss that wasn't there before. "Okay. We're both here."

"Hi!" Echo's higher, happier voice chimes in, sounding half-full of food. "Can I call you Elly May now?"

"As in Clampett?" I have to smile. "Um...no."

Echo's laugh is something approaching a snort. "You've got to admit, that was funny."

"I don't have to admit that any more than you have to admit the remark was juvenile," I tease.

"Spoilsport." I can picture her sticking her tongue out at me.

"Whiny brat," I jab back because that's what older sisters do.

"Whatever..." She scoffs at me. "So how are the wilds of North Carolina?"

"Nice, but hardly wild. Charlotte has, like, almost a million people, so it's not a rural middle-of-nowhere. It looks like a city, but it has a different sort of charm than home."

"Any *Gone with the Wind* mansions or cowboy hats?" She sounds as if she's eagerly waiting for me to say yes.

I roll my eyes. "Not that I've seen. But maybe you can look for yourself."

"What do you mean?" Eryn cuts in. "Do you need us to come there and help you?"

"I was hoping you'd hold my hand," I say in my calmest big-sister voice. "I'm getting married in two weeks."

"What? Are you fucking kidding me?" Eryn spits out.

"That's so romantic! It must have been love at first sight." Echo sighs.

"Actually, we met six months ago." I don't say more. What are the odds that my cautious response will prevent Eryn from asking more questions?

"If you were seeing someone seriously, why is this the first we're hearing of this?" Eryn asks suspiciously. "How did we not know about him?"

"When we met, I was on a date with a friend of his. He moved out here soon after that. But he called me recently to tell me he'd never forgotten me...and here we are." That's as booby-trap free as I can make that explanation, but I rattle on, mostly to shut Eryn up. "His name is Carson Frost. He inherited a candy company called Sweet Darlin'."

"Oh, my god! They make the Eversweet Chewy Pop." Echo sounds excited. "It's literally my favorite."

"There's so much sugar in those," Eryn points out, sounding just shy of scolding. "Focus, Echo. What's the hurry to get married, El? If you've only been with him for a few days, it's even too soon for you to know if you're pregnant."

"That's not why we're getting married. It's a long story, and I'll tell you all when you get here. Carson and I are sending you tickets to fly here for the wedding, so—"

"Wait," Eryn cuts in.

"Yeah, hold up. He lives in North Carolina?" Echo jumps in. "You're going to be moving there?"

"I'll explain when I see you. Just make sure you both clear the time off with work. Echo, you might miss a day or two of school."

"For you, that's nothing," she assures me. "I just want you to be happy. Are you sure this is what you want?"

No. But Gregory Shaw is a shark who came baring his teeth today, and I can't leave Carson out in the water, bleeding like chum, without a life raft. I love him too much.

I don't know what will become of us. If we want to be together, one of us is going to have to sacrifice something deeply meaningful. If we part ways, my sisters will be taking me home with them, most likely brokenhearted.

Maybe I should have stepped back and not gotten so involved with Carson. But holding in my feelings isn't in my nature. I'm so drawn to him that I looked at the man, saw his smile...and fell.

"Yes. You'll be my bridesmaids, right?" I close my eyes and feel tears seep down my cheeks. I imagined asking them that question to the tune of squeals and hugs and huge smiles on all our faces while showing off the sparkling diamond on my hand. But the lies feel so terrible, and I don't think I'm capable of sounding ecstatic right now. I'll settle for solemn and pray they interpret my quiet as me feeling the gravity of the situation. But if they could see my face, the jig would be up. Despite my being an actress, Eryn and Echo know me too well for me to hide much from them.

And I'm terrified that I don't have long to figure out how I'm going to act my way out of this snarl. If I can't, the ploy will be over before the wedding has even started.

"Yeah. Sure," Echo vows to me.

Eryn takes longer to respond. "You know I'd do anything for you, but I need to meet this guy before he takes my sister from me."

She doesn't sound thrilled. I understand. If Carson and I find a way to be together after this wedding fiasco, I might have to give up the only home I've ever known. It's pretty here. Charming...but different. Where will I work? What about my aspirations? And what will I do without my sisters?

"That's the plan," I say.

"Are you telling Mom and Dad?" Eryn asks.

"I will, but I don't think they'll come."

"Sorry, sis," Echo says softly. She doesn't even try to tell me I'm wrong because I'm not.

Suddenly, Carson opens the door to the office and drags in a big breath. I can't read his face except that he looks a little shocked.

"Can you two each bring a black dress when you come? We don't have time for bridesmaids' gowns now and—" Carson glances my way like he's a man with something to say. "Hey, let me call you later. I need to talk to my fiancé." It feels so weird saying that...but I better get used to it—at least temporarily. "He just walked in the door."

"Where was he?" Eryn quizzes.

I could have lied that he was running errands or something, but I'm already in that pit too deeply. "I'll get the plane tickets situated and let you guys know the details, okay? I love you both. Bye for now!"

"Bye. Love you," Echo says.

"Damn it, Ella. I don't understand—"

I hang up on Eryn and let out a shaky breath.

"Your sisters?" he asks. "How did they take the news?"

"About how I expected. Echo is seeing visions of me in a Scarlett O'Hara-type wedding dress, walking down the grand, sweeping staircase of Tara toward a southern version of Prince Charming. Eryn wants to know if I've lost my mind." I sigh. "It'll be fine... eventually."

"I'm sorry this is rough on you." He grabs my hand and squeezes it. "And your family."

"Thanks. How did it go with Kendra?"

"She's really happy for us. She's going to drop her ring off at my office sometime this week. Then that will be that." He rubs at the back of his neck and gives a self-deprecating laugh. "Actually, she couldn't wait to get off the phone with me so she could tell Brayden that she was a free woman."

"Does she worry that if she doesn't marry you her father will withhold her trust fund?"

He shrugs. "She says she's been giving that a lot of thought over the past couple of days. She's decided she doesn't care."

Kendra stating that she'd rather be happy than rich is not the reaction I expected. I thought she'd gladly give up her new ROTC boyfriend for all that money. Wealth is all she's ever known. Or is she simply hoping that she can wheedle and manipulate her father into backing down? I don't know if she's even more unrealistic than I've imagined or whether she's matured enough to stand on her own two feet because she finally found something that mattered.

"Interesting," I finally murmur. "I guess that's good for us. And for her."

"I hope so. I also called the head of the charity, Roger Clarke, and told him about you. He's more than happy to have you join the organization." Carson rattles off a salary that's not cushy, but more than I expected from a nonprofit. And certainly more than I was making back home. "Roger said that he and the rest of the staff are taking Monday off to recover from Friday's benefit, but he'll look forward to seeing you on Tuesday morning at nine. I'll forward you his contact information, along with the office address."

"Perfect. Thanks." I'm actually excited to start this position, but at the same time I'm sad I won't be able to hang around long enough to really make a difference in the lives of the kids I'm supposed to be impacting.

As if he can read my thoughts, Carson assures me, "They'll be happy for whatever time you can give them. I promise, it will be fine."

I hope Carson is right, but he knows Roger Clarke better than I do, so I'll do my best to believe him. "All right."

"After that, I called Gregory Shaw and told him you and I will be getting married. He sent me the contact info for the wedding planner he hired. I met her once. Her name is Vasha. I'll text her number to you, as well."

"I'll call her and find out the details. I guess we at least need to know when to show up." Despite the weight of our dilemma, I have to laugh.

"The wedding is scheduled for August twenty-sixth at seven p.m. at the Aria. I know that much. But I don't have any of the other details."

When I start thinking about everything else wedding related, a light bulb goes off in my head. "I need a dress! I can't wear Kendra's." And I wouldn't want to. "We're not the same size."

Carson grimaces. "Can you find something in the next couple of days?"

Like that's a simple task? I've never looked for one personally, but I've watched *Say Yes to the Dress* for years. Choosing never looks easy. I don't really want to go dress shopping without my sisters. I'll feel alone and lost, trying to wade through a sea of tulle and satin by myself. Then again, it's not the dress I'm going to wear for the real ceremony at my forever wedding. I just need something that fits.

I scuttle the disappointment I have no business feeling. "I'll see what I can do."

"Do you want me to...come with you?" He must be making this offer strictly to please me, because he looks like he would rather pull out his own molars with a pair of pliers.

"I'll only get you involved if I'm striking out. How's that?"

He looks relieved. "Good. Call me when you find something. I'll come over and take care of the rest."

I nod. "My sisters will bring their own dresses. I hope two bridesmaids are enough for the ceremony they had planned."

"We'll make it work. I, um...haven't even asked anyone to stand up with me yet. But I should do that."

"Yeah." It already seems late. "Beyond that, I guess Kendra and the wedding planner should have everything under control. Right?"

"Everything...except this." Carson reaches into his pocket and pulls out a little black velvet box.

My heart stops. *Rings. Right.* I completely forgot about those.

When he opens the box, I see a simple but beautiful emerald-cut diamond set in white gold. The inside lid proclaims the gem is from Tiffany.

I gasp. "It's beautiful."

"It was my mother's. This is the ring Craig gave her when they got engaged."

With just two sentences, our fake marriage suddenly feels very real.

"Oh, no." Frowning, I take a step back. "I shouldn't be wearing that."

"Why not? You said you like it."

"I love it. It's elegant and timeless and..." I take a deep breath.

"But what I think doesn't matter. Your mother's ring means something. It should only be worn by the woman you truly intend to marry."

His face tightens as he watches me with softening blue eyes. "How do you know that won't be you someday?"

My response is instant. I go warm and gushy inside. It's so girly and stupidly, hopefully romantic, given the situation. I need to temper myself.

"But right now, do you really want to dishonor something so special with a lie?"

"Well, look at this as being practical. The ring is handy. Mom would understand. After all, she loved Edward enough to free him to be with Sweet Darlin' because he needed it more than he wanted her."

With two workaholic parents, I completely understand what he's saying. "Why didn't Kendra wear this?"

Carson hesitates. "It...didn't seem like her, and she wanted something in rose gold. But you wearing my mom's ring will make our engagement seem more real." He pauses and caresses my cheek. "Most important, I can't think of anyone else I'd rather see with it on her finger. Will you wear it?"

Something fluttery stirs in my stomach. Nerves. Excitement. I'm too afraid to call it anything else.

I look up at Carson, lost in his gaze. Some foolish part of me wishes he was proposing for real. Not that I'm ready to take that step with him...I don't think. God, I'm confused. Everything is happening so quickly. My brain is telling me to slow down, think smart, do whatever I can to mitigate the damage to my heart later.

My emotions are running wild, and every bit of me simply wants to say yes and fling myself against him, join with him. Stay with him.

Suddenly, I'm fighting the sting of tears, the trembling of my chin. "Are you sure?"

"Hey, don't cry, sweetheart." He leans in, kisses my forehead, my nose, my lips. He lingers there, not deepening the contact, just taking comfort from our closeness, as I am. "Please."

Without meaning to, he pries open my heart in a way I can't seem to stop. I can't say no. "I'll wear it."

And I already know the day I have to take it off and give it back will hurt so badly.

Carson smiles my way as he plucks the diamond nestled in the box. "Give me your hand."

This would be so much easier—and less real—if he didn't put it on my finger as if I were really his bride.

"That's okay. I'll do it." I hold out my hand to him, palm up.

He scowls as he spends a long moment glancing between the ring in his grip and the expression on my face. Finally, he sighs and gently sets it in the middle of my palm. The metal is cool against my skin. The diamond shines like white fire, brilliant and beyond lovely. As a symbol of eternal love, it's absolutely breathtaking.

"It's just under two carats, and my mother always said it was a joy to wear. It matched everything and connected her to the man she loved in a way that made her feel safe."

As I ease it onto my finger, I suddenly understand. It fits perfectly. In the right circumstance, its weight would be a subtle reminder of my groom's care and commitment. But this isn't real, and I need to keep reminding myself of that. "I'll take good care of it. I promise."

Carson takes my hand, looking a little choked up at the sight of his mother's ring there. "I know you will. It looks perfect on you, by the way. I have the matching wedding band in my safe, along with my stepfather's ring."

Breaking his gaze, I nod. I can't look at him anymore without wishing circumstances were different, despite how illogical that may be. If I don't change the subject or lighten the mood, I'm going to be sucked down into this whirl of hope, desolation, and yearning that hurts too much.

"I'll...um, call this wedding planner and leave her a message. Hopefully, she'll get in touch with me on Monday."

He nods slowly, as if he's reluctant to accept the change in subject. "How about on Friday we head down to the venue so we can see it together. We should also go apply for a marriage license since it's only a few blocks away."

I gulp. I suppose we have to go through the motions to make it look real, but... "Do we have to do it in person?"

"I assume so. I don't know for sure. Both Kendra and I were dragging our feet, so we never got around to it."

That doesn't surprise me. "I'll talk to the wedding planner, but you're probably right. I...um, guess Friday would be good. If Roger is all right with it."

He nods as if the matter is settled. But nothing else is. "You going to be all right, Ella? Is this too much for you?"

It can't be. He needs me. "I'm fine. It's just more emotional than I thought."

"It is." He hesitates. "But I'm here if you need anything."

"Space," I say finally. "I need some time to process all that's happened. Alone."

Carson gnashes his teeth and looks hesitant to leave me, but he nods. "I'll head into the office for a few hours so you can have the place to yourself. I'll pick you up about six for dinner."

"I'll be ready," I promise as he retreats into the bedroom to get showered and dressed.

I sit on the sofa, feeling shocked and overwhelmed and staring at the winking engagement ring on my hand, wondering how I'm going to make it through this without falling apart.

CARSON

Friday rolls around. The six days between the moment Ella and I got "engaged" and this afternoon have flown by. She's been settling into her new job and coming back to my place every night with a glow in her eyes and a smile on her face, talking about the great holiday programs for kids the organization has in store. They're even planning a rendition of *A Christmas Carol*, as well as story time with Santa every Saturday in December.

The past few evenings, we've been eating her healthy dinners and drinking wine while I listen to her excitement...only to see the light die from her eyes the moment she remembers she won't be around to witness any of her plans come to fruition.

The nights are, in some ways, worse. Oh, they're full of pleasure—desperate, ravenous, blistering ecstasy that's undoing me and bending my soul. I fall asleep in the wee hours of the morning panting, drenched, and completely wrung out...only to roll over again every morning and take Ella hungrily before I drop her off at work and head to the office myself. It's as if we both feel the countdown of the ticking clock and don't know how to stop it.

I glance at my computer screen. Why is it barely after one? Because I'm eager to be out of here, to see the venue where Ella and I will marry—or pretend to—while I try to think of some way to convince her that maybe we should consider exchanging vows for real. It's soon, I know. I don't want to rush her. She deserves to feel certain, and we'd have to talk long and hard about how we would be married when we live on opposite coasts. But I'm not ready to let this woman slip through my fingers. If I do, I'll be losing the best thing that's ever happened to me.

And deep down, I fear I'll be making an irrevocable mistake.

Suddenly, I hear a knock on my office door.

"Come in," I call. I may as well stop pretending I'm studying this spreadsheet, trying to draw any relevant financial conclusions.

The handle turns with a little click, and Cora peeks her head in, her silvery hair making her green eyes all the more vivid. "You have a guest. Kendra Shaw is here with a...friend. Are you available?"

She must be here to return the engagement ring I bought her. No idea what I'll do with it. eBay, maybe? I also have a suspicion I know who her "friend" is. This should be interesting...

"Show them in."

I try to close down the worksheet with sensitive financials, but the computer freezes and I can't seem to get the file saved before I hear Kendra's high-pitched, southern-flavored voice. "Hi, Carson."

I turn and swallow a curse, using my body to block my screen. I already know that Kendra has no interest in anything that involves Sweet Darlin'—or her father's company, Dulce Lama. She's not interested in business at all. But I know nothing about the hulk beside her wearing a uniform that bears a striking resemblance to dress blues. His hair has been shaved so short I can barely discern it's some sort of brown. He has dark eyes that observe everything and wears an expression that's no-nonsense.

"Hi, Kendra. You must be Brayden." I extend my hand in his direction.

He shakes it with a firm grip that's a tad too close to crushing for comfort. It's a subtle warning to stay away from his girl. I hold back a laugh. He has absolutely nothing to worry about from me.

"I am." His voice is as clipped and unwelcoming as his expression.

Kendra elbows him gently. "Brayden, Carson and I are..."

"Formerly engaged," he finishes Kendra's awkward incomplete sentence.

"That's true, but maybe a better description is that he's become a friend."

Now that we're not being forced to marry? "I like that. Yes."

Brayden scowls but accepts her proclamation in silence.

"Thanks for having the courage to end this," she says. "I should have months ago, instead of pretending to be so vapid. I kept living up to my father's unenlightened characterization of me, hoping you'd want out. I'm sorry. I should have simply refused." She curls her hand around Brayden's arm and glances up at him with a starry expression I've never seen her wear. "I guess it took finding the right person to make me realize I had to stop trying to please my father, start pleasing myself, and do the right thing."

Hold up. Her insipid antics were an act? "You're not a boy-crazy, dancing-topless-at-a-frat-house type?"

Kendra grimaces. "No. I made that up. I was getting desperate."

"I'll be damned. I did not see that coming."

She laughs. "It seems I had everyone fooled, except Brayden."

When she squeezes her fiancé's arm, I notice she's wearing a new engagement ring. The stone is a mere pinprick compared to the rock I'd previously given her, but this gem makes her far happier, I can tell.

I smile. "I'll say. So...what about all the losers your dad said you dated in the past? Were those strictly to annoy him?"

"I had to get my teenage rebellion in somehow," she quips. "By the way, Ella is beautiful. It was lovely to meet her at the benefit. Y'all look good together. I hope you two will be happy."

"Thanks. I hope you'll be happy, too. Speaking of..." I glance pointedly at her not-so-naked finger. "Do you have good news to share?"

Kendra flashes her new engagement ring, looking so proud and excited. "Yes. We're getting married!"

And I hear the squeal of an excited bride that I never heard from her when her father forced us together.

"That's fantastic. Have you set a date yet?"

The pair exchanges a glance, and Kendra pets his arm as if to silently ask for his trust. That piques my curiosity.

"We're on our way to the airport now," Brayden finally admits. "We're eloping to Vegas."

This is a conversation full of surprises. I'm stunned on multiple levels. "Congratulations." *I think.* "Didn't you meet less than two weeks ago?"

"I know it's fast," she rushes to assure me. "But...I looked at him and I knew. I'm sure you'll tell me that's crazy. Or you'll think I really am that flighty sorority girl my father foisted off on you. But it's not like that. I'm finally serious about life because I have a reason to be."

She turns her blue eyes up to Brayden, whose stoic expression finally breaks to reveal utter adoration. I don't know what shocks me more: that she might actually be in love or that this straightforward man with a military mentality is equally willing to reveal his love after less than two weeks.

"That's fantastic, Kendra. Congratulations."

"Thanks. Here." She digs into her purse and fishes around before she withdraws a red velvet box. She opens it to reveal the familiar cushion-cut solitaire with pavé diamonds set in rose gold.

I snap it shut and take the box back, then deposit it in a desk drawer—still blocking Brayden from viewing my screen. "I appreciate you returning it."

Kendra shrugs. "If I didn't want it because I didn't want to marry you, it didn't seem right for me to keep it."

Fair enough. "So...I take it your father doesn't know your weekend plans?"

She shakes her head. "I told him we were going camping in the Smokies and we might not have any cell service."

I nearly choke. "You, camping? No offense, but you're a princess who likes her creature comforts. Did he believe your cover story?"

"I don't know. I left him a voicemail and promptly turned off my phone. I'll call him on Sunday, after we're married. Then...I'll let the chips fall."

"He's already threatened to block you from your trust. What if he cuts you out of Dulce Lama altogether?"

She shrugs and looks at Brayden again, as if reaffirming the answer they've already discussed. "We'll survive. We may not have a lot of money. As soon as we graduate from college, my husband—oh, I love the sound of that—will be going to officer candidate school in Rhode Island. Then we'll be living wherever the military takes him. And that's perfect by me."

I frown and glance Brayden's way. "You don't have any interest in Dulce Lama, either?"

"I've known from the time I was four that I wanted to join the navy. My father was an enlisted man, and I sometimes tease him that I intend to outrank him someday. But corporate America isn't for me. I know nothing about making candy or running a multimillion-dollar organization." Brayden scowls, and for the first time, I see something on his face that tells me he's thought this through. "Money doesn't motivate me the way duty, honor, and country do. I already know Mr. Shaw will have a difficult time believing that, so Kendra and I drafted a legal document. We both signed it and had it witnessed. I can't ever touch a dime of her trust and I can't ever become involved in any part of her father's company should he leave it to her. Mr. Shaw may never accept me as a son-in-law and he may even think I'm marrying Kendra for a paycheck. After all, I came from nowhere anyone could find on a map, and the only thing my family has an abundance of is love. That's fine. He'll learn sooner or later that I'm marrying her because my world revolves around her. I intend to spend the rest of my life with her."

Weirdly, I actually believe them. Even weirder, I hope they make it.

I walk away from my frozen computer—it doesn't seem as if it matters if they see anything on my screen—and approach them. I shake Brayden's hand and drop a kiss on Kendra's cheek. "Good luck to both of you. Enjoy your wedding."

"What about you and Ella?" she asks. "Dad said that you two are going to use the ceremony I'd previously planned for us."

"More or less. You did a great job. We don't have time to change much since we're also in the midst of buying a house, but Ella and I talked to the wedding planner and made a few changes to the flowers and tablecloths to accommodate a more muted color scheme."

"Muted? You're so diplomatic. You mean Ella didn't want Barbie-pink?" Kendra laughs.

As she does, the truth dawns on me. "You did that on purpose?"

"I did. Every time I mentioned it, I noticed you either winced or tuned me out." She elbows me with a grin. "I'd really hoped the accent fabric with hearts and bows everywhere would be the perfect touch."

"Um..." I pull at the back of my neck with a wry grin. "I think when the planner sent the samples to Ella, her comment was something along the lines of 'everything's vomiting a six-year-old girl's fantasy.'"

"When I chose the material, Vasha tried so hard to talk me out of it," Kendra says of the wedding planner. "Glad to know she and Ella both are getting their way."

"Yes. We're going with a classic black-and-white theme."

"That sounds a lot more elegant and far more like you. But the venue is beautiful."

"We're seeing it in a couple of hours." And I hope when we do, my "fiancée" will be inspired to get married for real.

"Fantastic. Did Ella find a dress?"

"Actually, her middle sister almost got married a couple of years ago and still has the gown she bought. Eryn is going to bring it for Ella since we're on such a short timeframe."

Kendra nods. "If it will fit, that's handy."

"What about you? Wearing the one you already picked out?"

"No. I found a simple lacy white sundress on clearance at Neiman's that's exactly what I want and—"

"Baby girl, I hate to interrupt but we're going to miss our plane if we don't leave now," Brayden points out quietly.

She glances at her delicate wristwatch. "You're right. Oh my god, we've got to run. Next time you see me, I'll be Mrs. Brayden Ashmore. Bye, Carson." She hugs me one last time, and I hope the happiness she feels now will carry through the rest of her life. "I'll see you next weekend."

I hesitate. "You're coming to my wedding?"

Kendra flashes me a grin. "Absolutely. I wouldn't miss it for the world!"

CHAPTER NINE

ELLA

It's been a stressful week, and by the time Friday evening rolls around, I feel jittery and shaky and so confused. Today, I said the final goodbyes to my new coworkers. They don't know that yet. They won't until Monday. Leaving early has ripped me in two. I've really enjoyed the job for the two weeks I've had it. Yesterday, I got to meet some of the kids from one of the church groups the organization is helping. Their appreciation was touching and their excitement infectious. I feel like a phony shit for walking out on them all.

Worse, the phony trend will continue tomorrow. I'll be a fake bride. I'll fake smile for my fake wedding to Carson before I fake run out on him prior to reaching the altar. He'll fake being shocked and heartbroken, while I'll manufacture fake drama the whole tragic night before I truly slink off alone, probably to cry real tears.

Sunday morning, I'll be back on a plane with my sisters, winging toward my old life in Los Angeles, owing them a crap ton of explanations, and without the man I love.

I don't know if I can do it.

My sisters arrived yesterday. They both liked Carson

immediately, which doesn't surprise me. He's awesome—handsome, funny, charming when he wants to be. Eryn and Echo both have given a thumbs-up to Charlotte and said that if they had to part with me for a man, a new city, and a new life, they understand my choice.

I wanted to cry because I can see myself here, too. As Mrs. Carson Frost. Keeping my job and racing to the new home we toured last Sunday afternoon and loved. He put in an offer on the property Monday morning. We found out last night that the sellers accepted. I'm sadder than I thought I would be that I won't be living in that dream house with him. Someday, another woman will. I'm jealous of her already.

How would he react if I said I might want to stay?

"Are you ready for this?" Eryn sidesteps closer as we all mill around the empty ballroom, waiting for our wedding rehearsal to begin. The hotel is beautiful, and I have no doubt our "wedding" will be exquisite.

I give her my best fake impression of happiness. "Yeah. I'm excited."

She frowns at me. "You should be. He's great. Really. If West and I shared half the love you and Carson seem to, we might have made it to our wedding day."

I swallow down more guilt. Eryn rarely talks about her ex-fiancé anymore. Weston Quaid was a good guy, if a little rough around the edges. He seemed to worship her—right up until the end. "I think you did share love. Twenty was too young to get married, and he got spooked."

"Because he didn't love me enough." She gives me a tight grin as if she doesn't want me to candy-coat the truth. "But better to know that before we got married than after."

She's right, but that doesn't ease her pain. I have no doubt some part of her is still attached to West. "I know your wedding dress has sentimental value for you. Thanks for lending it to me."

"It was gathering dust in the closet, so I'm glad someone will finally put it to good use. We're lucky it didn't need more than a little hem and tuck for it to fit."

When I tried it on after the tailor rushed through the few alterations in the last twenty-four hours, it fit as if it were made for me. Even slipping the gown on was both a joy and a sorrow. With lacy straps that hug my shoulders, an embellished bodice that dips to show the right amount of cleavage, and a tulle skirt that's pure romance, it's perfect. Or it would be if I were actually getting married.

I'm so torn about this fake wedding. Honestly, I'm torn about my relationship with Carson in general.

"Okay, everyone in their places," Vasha calls out.

I spy him cutting up with his two groomsmen. Luis, one of the guys he went to college with, is darkly handsome and recently married. His other pal from a previous job, Sam, has a more cool, aristocratic appeal—until he smiles, which seems to be often. In fact, they're all laughing now, clinking booze in plastic glasses, looking as if they don't have a care in the world. When my "groom" slants a glance my way, I know instantly he's got something on his mind.

Nerves knot my tummy. I'm not sure which outcome to hope for anymore—for him to call off this farce right now or tell me he wants to make it real.

"I need my bride and groom," the wedding planner shouts, motioning me over with a flip of her hand.

I head toward her dutifully, dreading this pretense. Even looking at Carson now hurts. Making love is a bittersweet torture. It's impossible to believe that in twenty-four hours, I might see him again for the last time. Though we're in love, I'm worried it's not enough. What if we say we intend to make our relationship work from across the country? All right, but for how long? What event would change our circumstances? And what happens if one of us gets lonely or becomes frustrated that we can't be together? Or decides the deprivation isn't worth the effort anymore and calls to break up? Or maybe stops answering the other's calls and texts? I can't afford to fly across the country, and he can't spare the time away from Sweet Darlin'.

Once I leave, I don't see us working out. And that's killing me because I can't imagine living without him.

"Carson," Vasha calls again.

She might be five feet tall with long black hair and a round, youthful face, but looks are deceiving. This woman is as cuddly as a tigress. Everyone is a bit afraid of her—except Sam, who keeps eyeing her like he'd enjoy the chance to prove he can more than handle her claws.

Carson lopes in our direction. Vasha huddles us together and gives some instructions that barely register in my racing brain. He takes my hand and nods on our behalf.

"Great," the wedding planner says, snapping her fingers and signaling to someone we can't see to dim the lights.

The room falls silent.

"Bride and groom, tell your attendants what they need to be doing. I'm going to make sure the music is ready. Everyone must be in their places in five minutes."

With that, she's gone, focusing her considerable attention to some other detail I would never have even considered.

When I spin around to find my sisters and flub passing along whatever I didn't hear, Carson stops me. He wraps his hand around my wrist and sends me a searching stare. "You okay, sweetheart?"

I'm not sure what to say. "This is harder than I thought it was going to be."

"Being dishonest with Eryn and Echo? With everyone else?"

"Yeah." That's part of the problem, anyway. But certainly not all of it.

How do I tell him I have second thoughts about jilting him at the altar? He's hinted now and then that we might make more of our relationship someday, but he hasn't once suggested that we actually get married tomorrow. I don't want to presume he's interested in becoming husband and wife. Or ask, only to find out he's decided that's a no for him. But I think he still wants us together. He makes love to me every night like he can't stop touching me, like he can't breathe without me. I cling to him in sleep because I'm afraid I'll wake to find him gone. I don't want to be that woman who's too insecure to tell the man she loves that she wants more from their relationship, but I'm tripped up by my childhood. If my own parents couldn't really love me, why should this wonderful man? On the other hand, if I tell Carson I might want to be his wife for real and he wants that, too, someone will have to sacrifice so we can be together. Is either of us ready for that?

Why is this such a tangle?

"Talk to me," he says softly, taking my hand.

To everyone else, it probably looks like a tender moment between a couple ready to commit their lives to each other. But his worried stare is a demand that I fess up—fast.

"Not right now. Vasha is—"

"Being paid for her time, so she can wait a few minutes. This is about you," he insists. "Do you need some time alone? Or with me? Tell me. Whatever it is, I'll make it happen."

"Later," I promise. "This needs more than five minutes, and everyone is staring."

Carson glances around and realizes I'm right. He gives me a terse nod. I understand him well, so I know the jerk of his head isn't any frustration he has with me. It's annoyance on my behalf. He'd do most anything to make me happy...except give up the life he's worked hard to build. I'd do the same for him, which is why I'm standing in the middle of this massive ballroom about to practice saying an "I do" I won't utter tomorrow while I'm near tears.

"Definitely later. Whatever's upsetting you, we're going to talk it out."

I send him a thankful nod. He gives me a soft press of his lips.

The gentle gesture nearly bowls me over. It makes me want to hold on to him and never let go.

Suddenly, Eryn grabs my arm and leads me to the back of the room, by the double doors leading inside. "What is going on? You act like it's a funeral, not a wedding."

"It's just an emotional time." I don't point out that if she and West had made it this far, she would understand because, A, I'm lying about the whole situation, B, the reminder will only upset her, and C, it's not her fault that West left just before their wedding with nothing but a terse note and an apology.

"But the emotions should be happy."

Why is my middle sister choosing now to be sage instead of snarky?

"Lighten up, sis," Echo thankfully butts in. "I'm sure she'll be shitting joy tomorrow. Let her be a little worried and nervous tonight, okay?"

I grip her hand. "Thanks, brat."

"You're welcome, bitch." My youngest sister winks.

By now, someone has given Vasha a microphone, and heaven help us all. She starts barking orders like a drill sergeant. No one is safe.

"Okay, groomsmen, file in from this side door." She waits until Luis and Sam have sauntered across the low-shag carpet. Sam gives the pretty wedding planner a wink, which she completely ignores except for a roll of her eyes. "Now the groom..."

From the back of the room, I watch Carson approach his buddies. He'll do this tomorrow. He'll wait at the altar people have built for this sham ceremony and peer at the crowd with his counterfeit smile while they all stare back. I wonder how real his feelings will be. No doubt as real as my own.

I have to stop tripping over these maudlin thoughts. I've committed to this plan. I need to see it through.

Vasha calls my sisters up the makeshift aisle one at a time. She tells Eryn to slow her steps, then arranges everyone at the front, pointing out where standing flower arrangements and other items will be so no one trips. Finally, she motions me to begin my bridal walk. Shoving aside the thought that my procession now is the only time I'll actually reach Carson's side at the altar, I put one foot in front of the other, my heart physically aching.

Once we're all in place, the planner and the minister both give us a few reminders, then we're blessedly done.

Dinner is a subdued affair, and I'm sure it's because my mood is dampening everyone else's. Eryn and Echo flank me on one side of the table. Luis and Sam bookend Carson on the other, so there's no privacy for us to talk. Vasha begged off because she had too much to do. Carson's parents are no longer alive, and mine didn't come because they couldn't get away from work, as usual. There really was no time to invite out-of-town guests, so we're done with the lovely seafood restaurant and wine in under ninety minutes. I wish I could say I enjoyed it, but with every second that ticks by, I just want to crawl in bed beside Carson and cry that this night will probably be our last.

"All right, man," Luis slaps him on the back as soon as the check is paid. "Now you have to let us take you out for a proper bachelor party."

"Complete with strippers, booze, and regret," Sam quips.

"Yeah, sis," Echo chimes in. "You need one last partyfest before you become a boring married broad."

"Exactly. A few shots should help you face 'til death do us part," Eryn says with a salty expression.

"It's not bad at all," Luis says, defending his married state. "In fact, it's pretty damn wonderful."

My middle sister snorts. An argument ensues.

I glance Carson's way. He looks as enthusiastic about the idea of having one last rager with his peeps as I am, which is to say not at all.

"You know, guys, I don't need to stare at a stripper and shove bills into her G-string to feel as if my bachelorhood is complete. I just want to call it a night and spend it with my girl." He reaches across the table for my hand.

I grip it like a lifeline.

"Not acceptable," Sam shoots back. "Besides, we were going to splurge for your lap dance in the VIP lounge from Destiny Whipped Cream or whatever her made-up name is. Only the best for you, buddy."

"Thanks, but I'll pass," Carson drawls.

"Ella?" Echo asks.

"You know, I think I'd rather turn in, too. A bride needs sleep to look her best on her wedding day."

Eryn leans over and whispers in my ear. "Or maybe you need some sister time so you can talk about whatever second thoughts you're having."

If only. "I'm not. I just want to spend tonight with Carson. Do you need a ride back to the hotel?"

After we work out that Sam will take my sisters to the place they're all staying at in his rental, Carson and I dash out of the restaurant. I'm eternally glad he chose an eatery that's less than three minutes from his apartment.

As if by mutual agreement, we make nothing but small talk on the way, mostly about Vasha. He tells me that Kendra texted him some pictures from their elopement in Vegas. He hasn't seen or heard from Gregory Shaw to know what the man's reaction to the marriage is.

When we finally reach Carson's place, he opens the door with a quiet click and drops his keys. My heart starts to race. My palms sweat. I still don't know what to say. How far am I willing to go for love? Can I give up everything? Should I?

The second he shuts it, he turns to me in the dark and grabs my shoulders. "Ella?"

"I don't want to talk right now." I reach for the buttons of his shirt and start slipping them free, one by one.

He takes hold of my wrists to stop me. "I think we have to."

"Not yet. I need"—*to feel you one more time before we have a chat that might change everything between us forever*—"you."

Slowly, he releases me and nods. "All right, sweetheart. Because I need you, too. But we're talking afterward."

We exchange a glance for an uncertain moment. The silence hangs between us, and as I stare into his blue eyes, I can't imagine never being with him again.

Then, as if we can read each other's minds, we break the still at the same moment, each lunging for the other, arms outstretched, lips ready, hearts beating as one.

I attack the buttons of his shirt again as he grabs my face and tilts my head for a kiss that makes me shiver and robs me of thought.

"What are you doing to me?" he mutters as he comes up for air only long enough to search my face.

I don't know what he's looking for, but I'm betting it's connection, desire, and love—exactly what I'm looking for on his face.

"I could ask you the same thing," I pant.

"I used to be reasonable, logical, so damn sure."

I nod. "And everything feels crazy now."

"Yeah. Except for being with you." He thumbs my lower lip before he kisses me again.

Then we don't need words. Our lips speak them. Our fingers convey meaning. Our hunger translates what's in our hearts.

Carson peels away the sundress I wore to the rehearsal as I step out of my shoes. He unhooks my bra as I tear the crisp white shirt from the waistband of his slacks. We attack his fly together, his fingers focused on the fastening, mine on the zipper. The second he's open, Carson shoves his boxers down. I do the same with my lacy, barely there panties. He takes my hand, and I assume he's going to lead me to his bedroom. Instead, he pulls me closer, then bends and lifts me against his chest.

"What are you doing?" But I already know, and as much as I don't want to be affected by the romantic gesture, I totally am.

"Taking you to bed in my arms," he growls as he darts across the apartment in ground-eating steps.

I don't want to hurry through our last night. Some part of me wants it to last, but I need it to start now, go longer, stay with me forever...just in case.

When we reach the bedroom, he manages to have me on the mattress, flat on my back, before I can even blink. Next, he flips on the lamp, grabs a condom from the nightstand, sheathes himself, and crawls between my legs in the span of a single breath.

"Tell me you're wet," he demands, gripping his cock and positioning the head against my opening.

I shiver with thrill. "Drenched."

Some part of me wants to tease him, torment him with naughty suggestions I'd love him to make real, delay our gratification until we're both an instant from exploding. But we're already on the edge in our hearts. Our bodies won't be far behind.

"Good. I've got to have you. Right now."

That's all the warning I get before Carson reaches under my ass, lifts my hips to him, and drives inside me. I gasp when he's immersed deep, to the hilt. He sparks nerve endings that never quite go dormant when he's around.

The friction has me crying out and writhing beneath him. Carson knows my body so well now. He's learned it methodically over the past sixteen days. He knows how much I like to feel the sting of my scalp when he tugs at my hair, like he's doing now. He quickly discovered how much I love the little bites he nips up and down my neck when he's fucking me. He also figured out how crazy I go when his strokes are slow and controlled and a delicious torture because I have to wait for each and every one.

But I've learned him, too. Carson loves my nails in his back, my whispered words in his ears, and my legs wrapped tightly around his hips.

"You're so deep inside me." The words spill from my mouth. "It feels so damn good and I...ah. Yeah. That spot. There." As he drags over the sensitive area behind my clit with his cock slowly, I grit my teeth and sink my nails into his skin a bit more. "Carson, please..."

I know he likes to hear me beg, too. He knows how to make me plead for his mercy so easily. Sometimes, I try to fight him. Sometimes, I even succeed for a minute or two. But inevitably, like now, he drowns any resistance I have with a passion so consuming I can't muster the will to stop myself from beseeching him to give me the dazzling bliss only he can.

Every time between us is stunning and breath-stealing, but tonight it's as if he's so zeroed in on me—on us—that he delivers every stroke, every touch, every kiss precisely when and where I need it to surrender all of myself to him with dizzying speed.

"Fuck, Ella. Yes, sweetheart. This is... God, I need you." His strokes pick up speed and I can't hear his next words. His lips brush my neck, making me shudder in his arms. My heartbeat gongs in my ears. I'm only aware of the way he fills me, the way he overwhelms me, the way we're both bellowing for breath as we move together toward a pinnacle that will—shockingly—surpass all those we've shared before.

"Carson. Babe... More. Deeper. Please! Don't stop." My voice is a high-pitched cry as I'm perched on the edge of a climax that I know will undo me completely.

He digs his fingers into my hips. His methodical strokes deepen until I'm clawing and wailing, my body thoroughly electric and alive.

"Ella. Listen to me." He tugs my hair again until he snares me with his gaze. "You. Will. Not. Leave. Me." He punctuates each word with an emphatic thrust that leaves me no doubt how he's feeling.

I love him, too. My heart is alive and celebrating this one glorious moment, even though it's already bruised and weeping at the thought of what tomorrow will bring.

"Hear me?" he demands, pumping inside me furiously. "Tell me. Say it. Right now."

I'm torn. The words are on the tip of my tongue. I'm desperate to agree. Dying to, actually. I want to let myself commit to him in this moment so I can blame the pleasure he's using to coerce me later. If I promise him, I have to follow through, right?

But I don't speak. This is the rest of our lives, and we are adults. Plus, the ecstasy catches up to me before I can utter a word. It clutches my throat, seizes my vocal chords, and robs me of thought. I can only hold on to Carson tighter as I squeeze my eyes shut and unravel all the way down to my soul in a pleasure that's both sharp and burning...and yet exquisitely pleasurable. Carson's strokes pick up speed, igniting every nerve ending and tissue already swollen and on fire for him. He stiffens and grunts as he pours himself out. I keen for him until my throat hurts. Until I run out of breath. And still the ecstasy stretches on, almost vibrating inside me.

I open my eyes to him during this endless, timeless perfection. He's waiting, staring. I see love there—so much. The kind of steadfast, I'll-always-put-you-first devotion I've never had, especially not from my own parents.

Isn't this really what I've been searching for my whole life?

Finally, the grip of our mutual pleasure breaks, and we're left staring at one another, without breath, without words. Heartbeats and gazes speak for us. Besides, what can words convey now? We're in love. And we don't know if it will lead to anywhere except heartbreak.

He rolls to his left, taking me with him until I'm on top. I collapse onto his chest, arms around him. He clasps me tight. I don't know if it's the orgasm or the solemnity of the moment or maybe I can blame PMS. But I begin sobbing, falling apart in his arms.

It's not like me. I've always had to be the strong one for my sisters. I've always managed to keep them—and myself—going, even when the world might have looked dim. Right now, I only see the rest of my miserable life stretched out before me without Carson.

Who knew that taking a simple job to pretend to be his girlfriend for two and a half weeks would rip my soul in two?

"We have to talk about it, Ella," he says as he eases free and disposes of the condom.

"I know."

"I want you to stay with me. Keep your job. Move into the house I bought. Just...*be* with me."

His words tear my chest open and make me bleed. It's so tempting and yet so complicated. "You make it sound easy, like all I have to do is say yes. But—"

"I'm asking you to give up a lot, I know. Your aspirations, being near your sisters... We've talked through all that. But the problem goes deeper for you, doesn't it? What's really holding you back?"

I can't put it into words. A fear that I'll give up everything and somehow still be alone. My head is telling me that, with Carson, it's not logical. But what if I make the leap and he's so wrapped up in Sweet Darlin' that he forgets me? Loses interest in me? Drifts away from me? I'll be in an unfamiliar state without any family or friends of my own. I won't have my own space. I won't even have a job I secured by myself. Yes, I could simply pull up and move back to California, move near my sisters again and pick up the pieces. I'm not worried about where I'd live. I'm worried about the devastation to my heart.

What's Carson giving up to prove he's serious about us?

I don't want to doubt him, and some part of me knows the question is unfair. But I can't help how I feel. The emotions just...are. Trying to argue them away seems pointless. I know from experience they only come back until you figure them out.

That anxiety, the fear of ending up alone, is something I've never overcome.

"If that's really what you want, I need to think."

He nods. "Sweetheart, that ring belongs on your finger."

I've become so used to wearing it in the last couple of weeks its weight feels completely natural, even comforting. In fact, I have a terrible premonition that I'll feel naked without it. "When you first gave me this ring, it was purely for the purpose of outwitting Gregory Shaw."

"Things change, Ella. Do I still want to keep him from getting any deeper into my company? Of course. Is that the only reason I want you to wear my mother's ring? Hell no. If I'm being honest, it never was. I've been hoping for a while that I could convince you to stay here with me."

My heart is in my throat. I shouldn't be surprised he feels this way. I probably suspected it deep down. Everything between us has been like lightning—fast and bright. We feel so right together. Meant to be. Which doesn't make any logical sense because we only had our first real face-to-face solo conversation sixteen days ago. Should we even be talking about our future, much less forever?

"What would we do with the wedding? Continue the jilting as planned, then say afterward that we've decided to live together and figure it out?"

"We could do that." He cradles my face in his hands. "Or we could go through with it."

"Actually get married?"

His blue eyes soften as he reassures me with the adoration in his gaze. "Exactly. We have a wedding, a minister, your family, my friends, a valid wedding license... The details are done. I don't know that we could have planned the event any better ourselves."

We couldn't have. I'm terrible at organizing such things, and despite the few things Kendra tossed in to needle Carson in the hopes he'd back out, everything is exquisite and elegant. It will be a wedding to remember, and Shaw certainly spared no expense. It's a dream come true.

But I don't know if it's really real—or lasting.

"And you're not saying that simply to pull the ultimate one over on Gregory Shaw?"

"What?" He jackknives up, nudging me to his side. "Is that what you think? Let me be clear. I love you. If I got to choose what happens tomorrow, I'd marry you and move you here with me so we could be together forever. But you have to want that, too. I can't want it enough for both of us." Suddenly, he's on his feet and snatching a blanket from the back of a nearby chair. "I'm going to sleep in the office. I think you need the time alone to decide what you want tomorrow to be. Think long and hard, Ella. Because I'm playing for real." He strides to the door. "Let me know what you decide."

Then he's gone, the click of the door the only sound to break the otherwise terrible silence. I sink to the mattress alone, in sheets rumpled by our lovemaking and smelling like sex.

He's right. I need to make decisions. How far am I willing to go? How much will he break my heart if I say yes and this doesn't work out? How much will I regret it if I don't try at all?

I curl up with the sheets. Tears come. It's going to be a long night.

CHAPTER TEN

CARSON

"Good morning. Don't mind us," Eryn proclaims as she bursts inside my apartment, clutching Ella's keys, while I'm in mid-pour of my first cup of coffee. "We're just barging in."

Echo is right behind her, a long braid swinging over one shoulder, and wearing a smile. "Yep. We swiped her keys from her purse last night so we can kidnap the bride."

Is she going to be my bride today? Or just an actress playing a role? I don't know and I wish like hell I did. Last night, I left her to think. It was the last thing I wanted to do. When I brought up getting married for real, I'd hoped she would simply throw her arms around my neck with a squeal and say yes. Granted, it wasn't the most romantic proposal ever. But I meant every word I said. I love that woman and I want to spend my life with her.

"Is she still in bed?" Eryn asks.

When I peeked in on her a few minutes ago after my restless night? "Yeah."

"Go wake her and get her packed up," the middle Hope sister tells the youngest. "I'll make a plan with the groom."

"Got it. She'd probably rather see my smiling face than your sourpuss scowl first thing in the morning." Echo flashes her a cheesy grin.

"Ha. My guess is that you can't get it done without me and you'll need the big guns." Eryn flexes her biceps.

They don't look like big guns at all, and I try not to laugh at her gesture.

Echo sticks her tongue out and hops around to the bedroom, disappearing inside with a quiet stealth I hadn't imagined from such a little ball of chaos.

"Coffee?" I ask Eryn.

"I'm good. You're not going to fight me?"

"Depends. Where are you taking her?" Because I'm worried Eryn isn't sold on me yet, and if she says she intends to take Ella back to Los Angeles, I will show her big guns—and one hell of a battle to go with them.

"The day spa. Sam let us borrow his rental. We're making sure her hair, makeup, and nails get done before this evening's ceremony. Since my mom and dad decided work was more important than their daughter's wedding, she has no one but us to be her support system. She has no one else to get ready with or help her into her dress. And she won't have anyone to walk her down the aisle." Eryn bites her lip. "My sister basically raised us, and she would never admit it but she has difficulty believing people will be there for her, that they'll put her first. No one ever has. She wouldn't let me or Echo do that because we were her responsibilities."

That tells me so much about Ella. She's mentioned her situation with her parents in not so many words. I knew they were absorbed with work. I knew she cared a lot for her sisters. It didn't occur to me that the emotional impact on her was so great...or that she'd have trouble believing I'm serious when I tell her I love her and will always be here for her.

She needs me to show her.

If she marries me today, she will have to sacrifice everything she knows, wants, and loves for something she's afraid to believe in. She will have to trust in me—in the two of us—so utterly that she's certain down to her bones.

Have I given her enough of myself for that?

"I understand. Thank you for making her situation clear to me."

Eryn's expression changes, actually softens. I sense that she doesn't show many people her emotional side. I also sense her feelings run deep. "I've never seen Ella in love. I don't know what's *really* going on here. My older sister is a lousy liar—at least to the people who know her well—and she's never mentioned the job she supposedly came here for, so I assume you have something to do with that. But let me tell you now, she really, truly loves you. If you're just using her for some scheme, you're going to break her heart and she will never trust anyone with it again."

Damn, Ella's middle sister is smart and has seen more than I hoped. I manage to keep my expression blank. "I very genuinely want to marry your sister. I've made that clear."

"I hear the tone of your voice. You think the ball is somehow in her court." She shakes her head. "It's still in yours, pal. If you really love her—"

"I do."

Eryn lets out a deep breath, her shoulders relaxing, her

expression opening. "Then you need to find a way to make my sister say yes when the moment comes. Echo and I will get her ready and there on time. The rest is up to you."

Message received loud and clear. Eryn is on my side...but only if I go the distance to prove I love Ella. I have to make the beauty I've only known for a handful of weeks believe that she is my world—now and always.

"I've got this," I say, though I'm not sure how else to prove my love. "Thanks."

She nods my way, then the bedroom door barges open. Echo emerges, carrying the newly altered wedding dress in a long gray garment bag, along with Ella's suitcase.

The latter alarms the hell out of me. "You're taking all of her things?"

"I don't know what she'll need," Echo quips. "Besides, she insisted."

My heart stops. Does Ella think she's leaving me for good? No. She can't. We're not done, just getting started.

Eryn's raised brow says, *I told you so.* Ella's insistence underscores the fact that I have to step up my game. Echo looks guileless and unaware of the undercurrent in the room. "Why don't you ladies wait for her in the car? I'll send Ella down when she comes out."

"Nope." Echo shakes her head. "I'm not stepping a foot out of here without my sister. If we don't keep her on schedule this morning, she'll be late for all her appointments."

"I'll make sure she's down in five minutes."

"Oh, I get it. You think you're going to sneak in a pre-wedding quickie, huh?"

"What?" I don't want to take Ella to bed now. Well, I do, but that's not uppermost in my mind.

"You're bold. I'll give you that. But—"

"Let's wait in the parking lot," Eryn cuts in. "Carson will send Ella down. He'll make sure she reaches the spa in plenty of time."

As she ushers Echo out the door with Ella's suitcase, Eryn slides me one last stare. She's giving me her vote of confidence and I better not fuck it up. I nod, then she's gone, shutting the door behind her.

"Morning," Ella says softly from the threshold of the bedroom a moment later.

God, she looks a little red-eyed and uncertain but still beautiful. Clean and soft and female. Almost glowing.

I know I don't have much time, so I cut to the chase. "Morning. I'm sure you spent a lot of time thinking last night, but if you need to talk more—"

"I...just cried." She sighs. "Then I was so tired that I fell asleep. It was a busy day, and even after a couple of weeks with you I'm not used to the Olympic-level sexual gymnastics."

"Last night was intense," I agree. If I play this right, I'll have the rest of my life to try to sate the seemingly never-ending well of desire for Ella, but right now is about us. "Talk to me, sweetheart. Let me help you."

"I have to think this through alone." She shrugs. "You and I have talked it over. I'm not sure there's much more we can say. Now I just need to decide where I see my future. That's not something you can do with or for me, no matter how much you want to. But I'll be thinking about it all day."

What she says makes sense until I realize she may not have an answer for me until she's walking down the aisle.

I scrub a hand down my face. "Can I do or say anything to—"

"No. This is on me now. But I know how to find you if I have questions or need to talk." She holds her phone in her hand. "I know that's not what you want to hear, but I can't lie to you and tell you I have the answers now. I'll do everything I can to find them by five o'clock. I don't think eight hours is too long to ask for so I can decide the rest of my life."

"It's not." I'm just frustrated as hell at being left out of the decision.

What can I do, say, give her to help her make up her mind?

I'm drawing a blank.

"I have to go," she murmurs. "I'll see you at the altar."

"How will I know...?"

Ella hesitates a long moment. "I don't even know if I'll be sure what I'm going to do until I start walking up the aisle. I guess we'll both find out then."

She brushes a soft kiss on my lips. I'm still sorting out whether it's full of "until later" or "goodbye forever" when the door shuts behind her.

Suddenly, I'm alone. And if I don't figure something out, I have a suspicion I'm going to be even more lost for the rest of my days.

I wish like hell my mom and Craig were still around. Getting married without them here is bittersweet. Not being sure if I'm tying the knot at all is far worse. I could sure use the sage advice they'd give me now. Hell, I would even settle for Edward's counsel. He might have been a self-absorbed bastard to live with, but from everything of his I've read, he had sound logic and a good ear.

In fact, I'll bet Edward was a driven, ruthless planner, very much like Gregory Shaw. Both were known as crafty men of common sense and wisdom. Of course, I can't talk to my rival. He's the reason I'm in this position to start with. I can't ask him for advice on sorting this situation out without confessing everything.

Sighing, I turn that thought over in my head once, twice. Hmm... Suddenly, I have an idea.

I reach for my phone.

E L L A

"You look beautiful." Eryn's dark eyes well with tears.

For a girl who almost never shows her vulnerable side, I know that seeing me in the dress she purchased with love for her wedding to West must be hard. But everything on her face tells me she means what she says.

"Thanks." I turn to look at myself in the mirror on the back of the hotel room door. The sight is almost a shock.

My dark hair has been wrangled into a low knot at my nape with curls framing my face and sloping down one shoulder. A braid circles my crown, making the perfect frame for the veil that falls to my feet, brushing the hem of the tulle skirt that parts in the front to reveal a beautiful swath of lace from décolletage to ankle. My makeup is perfect—lips rosy but not garish, dramatic black lashes and liner. Soft taupey-pink eye shadows soften the look. A blushing pink shade makes my cheeks appear naturally flushed, and a coordinating shade of highlight on the tops of my cheekbones has me positively glowing.

The colors all accent my pale complexion and give me a fragile, doe-eyed appearance.

Even if I'd had a year to conjure up precisely how I wanted to look as a bride, I couldn't have imagined anything more perfect than this.

"You look...wow." Echo smiles and cups my shoulder. "Really. Wow."

"For being my younger and not-as-gorgeous sisters, you guys look pretty okay, too," I tease with a wink, trying to lighten the mood. Echo has been asking me all day what's wrong. Eryn hasn't said a word, but I see her wheels turning.

I don't want them knowing anything. I don't want to lay my decision at their feet. It's not their fault and not their problem.

"I need a pic of us all dressed up and looking like fine bitches," Echo insists.

We snap a couple of selfies, some serious, some goofy. For a moment, I forget that I'm still not sure whether I should gamble everything for a love this new and believe that Carson won't let work and whatever else he deems important swallow him up...or do the sensible thing and go home to Los Angeles and resume my life as it was.

A soft knock followed by a feminine murmur tells me Vasha wants in. "All ready?"

Eryn opens the door. "We are."

"You've got about five minutes. Carson and the groomsmen are waiting to get into position for the ceremony. The string quartet is playing soft music to entertain the guests who have filed in. Everything looks perfect. I double-checked each detail myself."

Now she's come to inspect me. She doesn't say that, but I get the message.

After checking my zipper, my shoes, and my teeth to make sure they're free of lipstick, she ushers us all out of the dressing room and down the hallway. Other hotel guests stare as we make our way to the closed double doors outside the ballroom.

"Let's get this party started!" Vasha says as she clasps the handle. "Don't forget. Echo, you enter when I motion to you. Eryn, you slide in behind her, hang at the back, and wait for my cue. Ella, you'll hear the music change, then the double doors will open for you. That's when you walk your way down the aisle to the man you love, right?"

I nod.

"Go get in position, ladies. The bride and I will be right behind you."

My sisters hug and kiss me, both looking misty-eyed and beautiful, before they line up at the massive entrance to the ballroom.

Vasha pulls me aside. "Got any last-minute questions?"

Um, should I actually marry the groom?

I manage to shake my head. "I'm fine."

"You're nervous as hell," she corrects, taking me apart with her gaze. "I'll tell you something... I've been doing this for ten years. I can usually tell within the first hour of meeting a couple whether they're going to stay married or not. I knew Carson and Kendra were doomed. In fact, I told my boyfriend they wouldn't make it until their wedding day. I was not surprised when Mr. Shaw told me there would be a change in bride for this ceremony. The first time I saw you with Carson, I knew your love would last. I see a lot of brides and grooms who are just infatuated, but you two have that certain something. It's right. I can feel that you're in love. So don't be nervous. You two will have a great life together. Now go be happy."

When she eases into the ballroom, I wonder if that's a preplanned speech designed to nudge hesitant brides into taking their walk down the aisle. I have to admit, it's pretty effective. On some level, I believe what she's saying. I don't doubt that I love Carson or that he loves me. But I'm not sure we'll withstand the long test of time—the years that lead to decades, children, jobs, stress, mortgages, and whatever else life has in store. How well do we really know each other? I'm not sure I'm secure enough in his feelings to take a leap and risk being left behind.

I cringe. I sound like a scared little girl. I hear the whine in my own head. I still think like the nine-year-old girl whose mother pressed a house key into her palm and told her to walk her sisters home from school. To make sure they got something to eat because she was working late and Dad was out of town on a job. I did everything she asked. I helped Eryn and Echo take baths and I tucked them into bed. Then I fell asleep on the sofa waiting for my mother. I woke up the next morning with a crick in my neck and found my mother slumbering in her own bed. She hadn't bothered to wake me up to put me in mine or even tell me she was home.

That scenario repeated itself over and over until we all got used to fending for ourselves. Being further down on my parents' priority list shouldn't matter now that I'm an adult. It shouldn't affect my romantic relationships. It does. I don't trust people, and I've sometimes looked for anything that resembled love without considering the quality of the man. But this time, it feels as if he's the real deal.

Still without knowing what I'm going to do, I step up behind my sisters, holding my bouquet in a trembling grip.

Suddenly, Vasha opens one of the doors and motions Echo inside. It's Eryn's turn next, and she cups my shoulder, silently telling me to do what's in my heart, before she disappears into the ballroom, too. Then I'm standing alone in the hallway, hearing the faint strains of classical music through the wood and shaking so hard I can barely stand upright on my heels. I think of the six times Carson tried to call me today...and the six times I didn't answer. What would he have said if I'd picked up? Would it have made any difference? Would I be less confused now if I had?

When the double doors open again, the wedding planner motions me in, her expression soft with understanding. "Carson is nervous, too. Take a deep breath. Enjoy your wedding day."

"Sure." I nod absently.

"Look on the bright side. I don't feel compelled to give you the speech I give lots of other brides that marriage doesn't have to be permanent, and I know the names of great attorneys..."

She's right—in theory. But I'd rather be scared and single than bitter and divorced.

Great attitude, El.

The music chimes five times, then swells. Hundreds of faces I don't even know stand and rise and turn to watch me walk toward an uncertain fate.

I'm stuck on the threshold, unable to take a single step. I definitely don't know if I can make it all the way up the aisle, only to runaway-bride it back down. I haven't even moved and I see expressions ranging from curiosity to judgment on the guests' faces.

What the hell am I doing?

Then I spot Carson at the altar, standing under an arch of white flowers, looking extremely handsome in his tuxedo. I see the tension on his face, the need. Just the sight of him wills me closer, gives me the courage to put one foot in front of the other and start my way between the makeshift rows of white folding chairs with their elegant black bows decorating each back.

I'm dizzy and everything feels surreal as I waltz my way forward. Thirty feet from the altar, then twenty, then ten... On my right, someone clears his throat. I turn my head and spot Gregory Shaw looking at me with a dare in his eyes. He doesn't think I'll go through with this. His smirk says I'd be stupid not to, but my loss is his gain. Is the man just waiting to pounce on Carson? Salivating to steal another chunk of Sweet Darlin' from my man? I don't want to let him win.

Beside Shaw, Kendra and her new husband clutch hands, giving each other a secretive smile. Then her soldier turns to look at the front again, expression stoic. Carson's former fiancée turns her blue eyes on me and gives me an encouraging smile, a silent nudge that I can do this.

God, I'm even more confused now. What's the right decision?

With the music filling my ears, I turn my attention back to Carson. He's waiting for me, willing me toward him. I don't want to risk him leaving me...but how will he feel if I run out on him? Once, that's what we'd schemed. But now I think he'd feel terrible. Awful. Brokenhearted. All the things I'm desperate to avoid.

Five feet from the altar, I stop, frozen. No matter what I do, I'm risking someone's pain and disappointment and suffering. I don't want to mock marriage or lie through wedding vows when our parting may come much sooner than death. But I also can't imagine never seeing Carson again, never kissing him, never feeling my heart against his.

Behind me, I hear the rising murmur of the crowd. They're beginning to talk. They're wondering why I won't go the last yard and a half to my groom's side and speak my vows. They're speculating I have cold feet. They're whispering that this last-minute change of brides was hinky and how sad it is that Carson's first fiancée deserted him and now it looks as if the second might as well.

I close my eyes. I have mere seconds to decide. And I'm lost.

Until I feel warm, solid hands wrap around mine.

With a little gasp, I open my eyes to find Carson cupping my fingers, which are still clutching the bouquet. The moment our eyes meet, I see his heart. And I see my future. Despite the odds, sacrifices, and hardships ahead, I want to marry this man. I love him, the new house he bought, my new job, and the family we'll someday make. I will miss my sisters, but they're grown. They'll move on. Hell, they already have. And the devotion this man has given me in the last seventeen days is more important—and fulfilling—than any public adoration I might have received if I'd ever made it big as an actress. An Oscar won't fill the hole in my heart the way he does. I've barely thought about that—or my diet—in the last week. And I've been happier than ever.

With Carson Frost is where I belong.

"I love you and I want to marry you," he whispers.

"You've said that before."

"Now I'm proving it." He withdraws a piece of paper from the pocket inside his tuxedo jacket and hands it to me.

Around me, the strings are still playing, their hopeful notes swelling in my ears. The guests are now muttering amongst themselves in less-than-hushed tones. Vasha is staring at us from across the room, just outside the altar, scowling at our exchange.

I scan the document. It's simple but looks official enough. I read the text...but the meaning isn't sinking in. This can't be right. "You and Shaw made an agreement that if I walk away now, he gets the five percent you agreed to in exchange for the loan?"

"Yes. But if I ever leave you, divorce you, cheat on you, or otherwise make you unhappy for the next twenty years, he gets Sweet Darlin', free and clear. I leave with nothing."

"H-How?" With this agreement, obviously. That's not the right question. "Why?"

"I confessed our entire scheme to him this morning and then I signed that paper for you. Eryn explained your parents to me. I want you to know I'm never leaving. I will be with you and here for you every single day, forever."

The enormity of what he's done to prove his love and devotion to me sends shockwaves through my body. My eyes water. My hands begin to shake even more. I stare at the man I love, and I'm more sure than ever what I should do.

Crowd be damned, I throw my arms around him, stand on my tiptoes, and kiss him as if I'm beginning the rest of my life. Because I'm pretty damn sure I am.

"Um, you two... We haven't come to that part of the ceremony yet," Sam quips.

The guests laugh. I turn to my sisters and find them grinning widely, joy all over their faces.

I beam back at them and take my fiancé's arm. Together, we

walk the last few steps to the altar and join our lives.

The ceremony is a blur of words and faces. I'm glad the photographer and videographer are capturing everything because it's all spinning by—except when we speak our vows. That moment I look into Carson's eyes, time slows and I know we're going to be ecstatically happy together.

And I wish like hell we'd planned a honeymoon now. I saw an internet ad for this great new bed and breakfast right on the coast of Maui that sounds amazing. Maybe I'll bring it up to Carson once we get settled in the new house.

We slide rings on each other's fingers and the minister says a few more words before pronouncing us man and wife. When we kiss officially for the first time as a married couple, I feel joy speed through my body, ooze out my pores, saturate every moment between us.

We may have started with a fake relationship for all the wrong reasons, but what Carson and I have now is so real.

Suddenly, the guests clap. The minister introduces us as Mr. and Mrs. We run down the aisle together, hand in hand, to start our glorious new future.

I'm still grinning nonstop and loath to leave Carson's side as we sign our marriage license, take photos, and greet everyone who comes through the reception line. By the end of the night, my feet ache from standing and my cheeks hurt from smiling—and I'm still the happiest I've ever been. I'm now Ella Frost, married to a man who genuinely loves and understands me, working for a great charitable organization, living in a new city I can't wait to make my own, on the precipice of a future richer and more loving than I ever imagined.

We dance and eat dinner, slice cake and toast. The cocoon of sublime happiness is almost more than I know how to process, but I'm doing my best to bask in every moment so I can remember it for the rest of my life.

The deejay blasts a romantic ballad over the speakers. My husband claims me for another dance now that the crowd has begun to thin out. "Can I tell you how happy I am that you said yes, Mrs. Frost? I'm also glad I listened to Eryn this morning and followed my instinct to call Shaw. I knew I needed to convince you and—"

"I was already convinced," I murmur.

"You were?" Surprise widens his eyes. "You were going to marry me even before I told you about my deal with Shaw?"

I nod. "I'd decided I would take a leap of faith about five seconds before you told me what you'd agreed to. It wasn't strictly necessary, but it was a beautiful gesture. And it definitely sealed the deal. It gives a lot of comfort to know we're married and there's nothing you can do to change that."

When I wink, he laughs. "Not a damn thing."

"It also gives me tons of power. Now I can torment you in bed all I want."

"You can. In fact, I dare you. It will be my job to make you burn right back. And to love you with my whole heart because I intend to keep you sublimely happy, wife."

"I'm looking forward to that, husband." I brush soft fingertips across the back of his neck, just above his collar. "I'll give you equal bliss."

"Hmm. I can't wait. I'm definitely ready to get out of here and make love for the first time as husband and wife."

I want that, too. I look around to gauge crowd size, see if we can make our exit without making too many chins wag.

Instead, I see Gregory Shaw saunter over and tap Carson on the shoulder.

"You cutting in?" he asks the older man.

"No. I'm heading out...after I come clean." He glances across the room, where Kendra and Brayden are kissing quietly in a dark corner, obviously more than happy with their decision to elope.

I wonder what Carson's rival is talking about. *Come clean*?

"What do you mean?" my new husband asks.

Gregory Shaw sighs. "I haven't told Kendra yet. That's next on my agenda. On Tuesday I'm having surgery. The doctors think I have a benign brain tumor, but they won't know for certain until they remove it and send it to pathology for study. It's a risky surgery. I may not make it out. If I do, there's a possibility I'll never be the same again." He lets out another breath, as if admitting all that was hard.

I'm staring at him, utterly stunned. He looks so robust, still in the prime of his life.

Carson looks dumbfounded, too. "I had no idea. I didn't—"

"No one did, by design." Shaw jerks his head. "I wanted to keep it that way while I found someone who could run Dulce Lama in the event I didn't recover. I was hoping that someone would be Kendra's husband, but when you got cold feet...things got out of hand. But you were still my best candidate. I simply needed to test you, see if you could handle adversity and would fight for what you desired and believed in. Today, you proved to me exactly who you are. This is yours."

Carson takes the document Shaw offers with his proffered hand and unfolds it. "A power of attorney?"

"Yes. You'll take charge of Dulce Lama until I'm capable of returning. If I don't...the company is yours."

"You're signing it over if you can't serve as its CEO? Outright?" Carson looks astounded as he clutches the papers in his hand. "To me?"

Gregory Shaw nods. "With a few stipulations. I've reserved twenty-five percent of the annual profits for Kendra for the rest of her life. I'd like another ten percent to go to a charitable foundation that studies brain tumors. It's outlined in the document. The rest is yours to do with as you see fit." Then he gives us his signature smirk. "Of course, that's if I never make it back. But you should know, I'm planning to be behind my desk, giving you hell in the marketplace, in six to eight weeks. The competition is good for you."

Finally, Carson smiles. "You're right. I'll hold down your fort until then. Whatever you, Kendra, or Brayden need during this difficult time—or ever—all you have to do is ask. Today, you were like the father figure I no longer have. I appreciated the ear and the sage advice."

"And you were like the second kid I'm glad my wife never birthed," he jokes for a moment as we guffaw and chuckle. Then he sobers again. "I'm glad you're happy and that everyone got exactly what they wanted out of this situation. Good luck...son." Then he turns to me. "How about you, pretty lady? How does it feel to be staying here, married to this guy? I'll bet when he hired you to be his girlfriend, you never imagined you'd end up his wife."

"Never." I laugh. "Even though I've been an actress and I've played a lot of characters, I couldn't have conceived of a better ending, and I'll always relish the role of Carson's bride. I expect it to last a lifetime."

Gregory Shaw shakes my husband's hand and wraps me in a fatherly embrace before he excuses himself with a polite goodbye.

A few minutes later, Carson and I dash out of the reception to the sounds of cheers, party horns, and catcalls. I hug each of my sisters on my way to the waiting car. Carson pumps each of his groomsmen's hands in thanks before he clasps mine again. Then we sprint into our waiting limousine and drive off to start the best future ever.

MORE MISADVENTURES

ALSO FROM SHAYLA BLACK

More Than Want You

Keep reading for an excerpt!

MORE THAN WANT YOU

More Than Words: Book One

A NEW sexy, emotional contemporary romance series ...

I'm Maxon Reed—real estate mogul, shark, asshole. If a deal isn't high profile and big money, I pass. Now that I've found the property of a lifetime, I'm jumping. But one tenacious bastard stands between me and success—my brother. I'll need one hell of a devious ploy to distract cynical Griff. Then fate drops a luscious redhead in my lap who's just his type.

Sassy college senior Keeley Kent accepts my challenge to learn how to become Griff's perfect girlfriend. But somewhere between the makeover and the witty conversation, I'm having trouble resisting her. The quirky dreamer is everything I usually don't tolerate. But she's beyond charming. I more than want her; I'm desperate to own her. I'm not even sure how drastic I'm willing to get to make her mine—but I'm about to find out.

This book is the first in the More Than Words series. The books are companions, not serials, meaning that backstory, secondary characters, and other elements will be easier to relate to if you read the installments in order, but the main romance of each book is a stand-alone.

This book contains lines that may make you laugh, events that may make you cry, and scenes that will probably have you squirming in your seat. Don't worry about cliffhangers or cheating. HEA guaranteed! (Does not contain elements of BDSM or romantic suspense.)

★ ★ ★

After lingering for a few moments, I have to pull away. I'm not ready to break our connection, but the damn rocks are killing my knees. While she rises, I find a trash can beside the nearby towel stand and do away with the condom. When I turn back, I expect to find her dressing.

Instead, she's run stark naked into the water.

I'd ask anyone else if they were crazy, but Keeley flips a laugh at me over her shoulder, like she knows I'm wondering what the fuck she's doing. Instantly, I see a bright happiness beaming from her face. Since that's what she wants out of life, I feel good. Weirdly content.

"Come in the water," she calls to me.

"I'm not skinny dipping in the ocean. What if someone calls the cops to say there's more than one moon shining on this beach?"

Her laugh this time is heartier. "Then we sweet-talk our way out of it or go to jail, but how many times in life will we have the chance to do something like this?"

Probably not very many. She has a point.

I shuck my shoes and pants. "I must be crazy. I blame you."

"Good." Keeley turns to me, flashing me a full frontal of her glorious nudity. "You should."

I just had a monster climax less than five minutes ago, but I'm already hoping my recovery time is short. I'd love to get her back to the condo, into my bed, and do every crazy, dirty, wonderful thing to her I can think of.

"I will," I promise as I head into the brisk Hawaiian water.

Her smile—whether she means it or not—looks sultry. "I love

being a dangerous woman."

Though she sometimes seems so sweet I could get a cavity, I sense her wild side just under the surface. The male animal in me wants to feel her again. Tame her—at least for an hour or two.

I take her hand. With the other, she bends to splash me.

"You want a fight?" I challenge.

"Maybe..."

She's flirting. I love it. I'm never playful after sex. Most of my partners get their clothes on and leave, which is a relief. Tiffanii always showered the smell of sex—of me—off her body before she rolled over and went to sleep. In fairness, as a flight attendant, she often had to be up by four to work the 6:30 a.m. flight to Honolulu. Still, it pissed me off.

But Keeley wants to...frolic. I can't think of a better word. She's splashing and giggling and enjoying life.

It's contagious. I smile and splatter her with water in return.

With a sigh, she falls against me, still grinning, then steals a kiss. She's gone before I can pull her in closer, staring out at the vast ocean again.

I sidle up behind her and wrap my arms around her. My lips fall to her shoulder. She's the perfect height for me to press kisses there. She shivers in my arms.

"If you don't stop making me happy, how are you ever going to get rid of me?"

"Who says I want to?"

She scoffs. "Oh, I know your type. If you're too busy to come home and take advantage of this view, you're too busy for a relationship. It's okay. I get that you want satisfying, not meaningful."

A few hours ago, I would have agreed with her. Now I don't know what the hell is going on. An impulsive side of me I would have sworn didn't exist is telling me that I should try to make something of my connection with this girl. Keeley is interesting. She holds my attention. She's not into herself—her life, her parties, or her looks. She's into the people around her. She's into living. She makes me look at my life differently. Come to think of it, she's everything I've never had in a woman before.

If Britta truly knew this woman, my assistant would approve.

But Griff, the thirty-million-dollar listing, and the task I need to ask of Keeley tomorrow loom. I want to keep her with me longer... but my brother will lose his shit when he meets her. He'll fall all over himself to win her. He'll half-ass the Stowe estate to be with her. Doesn't that sound stupid? But trust me, it's true. And once the Stowe heirs see he's too busy chasing tail to chase leads, they will cut him loose. Then *bam*, I'm in. It's gold. I'll celebrate.

But I'll be celebrating alone.

Well, not exactly. I'll have Rob and Britta. They'll make a pretty penny from this deal, too. And I'll find another woman to make me feel good again, right? Now that I know how important personality and a carefree spirit are, I'll look for those qualities.

"I may surprise you yet," I tell her.

Not with the meaningful relationship stuff. Although...I wonder if there's any chance she'll agree to distract Griff and continue to sleep with me.

That sounds bad, I know. I probably shouldn't even consider the possibility. I'm worried about asking, too. I've seen what she can do to a man's gnads. It makes me shudder.

"Really?" She turns in my arms and smiles. "I think I'd like that.

Continue Reading in More Than Want You!

ALSO BY SHAYLA BLACK

Falling in Deeper
Dirty Wicked: Novella
Holding on Tighter

The Devoted Lovers
Devoted to Wicked: Novella
Devoted to Pleasure (Coming Soon)

Sexy Capers
Bound And Determined
Strip Search
Arresting Desire: Hot In Handcuffs Anthology

The Perfect Gentlemen
(by Shayla Black and Lexi Blake)
Scandal Never Sleeps
Seduction in Session
Big Easy Temptation
Smoke and Sin

Masters of Ménage
(by Shayla Black and Lexi Blake)
Their Virgin Captive
Their Virgin's Secret
Their Virgin Concubine
Their Virgin Princess
Their Virgin Hostage Their Virgin Secretary
Their Virgin Mistress

Their Virgin Bride (Coming Soon)

Doms of Her Life
(by Shayla Black, Jenna Jacob, and Isabella LaPearl)
The Complete Raine Falling Collection
One Dom To Love
The Young And The Submissive The Bold and The Dominant
The Edge of Dominance

Heavenly Rising Collection
The Choice (Coming Soon)

The Misadventures Series
Misadventures of a Backup Bride

Standalone Titles

Naughty Little Secret
Watch Me
Dangerous Boys And Their Toy
Her Fantasy Men: Four Play Anthology
A Perfect Match His Undeniable Secret: Sexy Short

Historical Romance

(as Shelley Bradley)
The Lady And The Dragon
One Wicked Night

Strictly Seduction
Strictly Forbidden

Brothers in Arms: Medieval Trilogy
His Lady Bride (Book 1)
His Stolen Bride (Book 2)
His Rebel Bride (Book 3)

Paranormal Romance

The Doomsday Brethren
Tempt Me With Darkness Fated: e-Novella
Seduce Me In Shadow
Possess Me At Midnight
Mated: Haunted By Your Touch Anthology
Entice Me At Twilight
Embrace Me At Dawn

Find all of these titles at ShaylaBlack.com!

ACKNOWLEDGMENTS

Though writing a book involves the author spending many hours alone with their computer, the finished product is the result of multiple people giving their time, dedication, and expertise to ensure the book is the best it can be when it reaches the reader's hands. As such, I have a cast of characters in my life to thank.

William and Baby Black – No matter how stressed, manic, sad, happy, or teary I get, you're there for every moment. Whether we're sharing the best of times...or not, I can count on you to hold my hand and give me a safe place in the world.

Rachel Connolly and Shannon Hunt – Thanks for being such integral parts of Team Black! You're great cheerleaders, organizers, and beta readers. But you're also amazing friends. Not much gets done without you two, so I can't tell you how much I appreciate you both. Oodles and bunches of hugs!

The amazing people at Waterhouse Press – Meredith, thanks so much for inviting me into this project. You said to write something fun, and I had a blast with this book! I can't wait to do it again. Scott, Robyn, and Shayla, you've all done your best to present this book to readers in its best possible form and you've been joys to work with. Thanks so much!

To my loyal readers – Many of you have been with me for years, some for decades. You've followed me from one series to the next and always supported me in whatever creative endeavor struck my fancy next. I appreciate you all for being the most awesome readers and some of the coolest chicks I'm happy to know.

ABOUT SHAYLA BLACK

Shayla Black is the *New York Times* and *USA Today* bestselling author of more than fifty novels. For nearly twenty years, she's written contemporary, erotic, paranormal, and historical romances via traditional, independent, foreign, and audio publishers. Her books have sold several million copies and been published in a dozen languages.

Raised an only child, Shayla occupied herself with lots of daydreaming, much to the chagrin of her teachers. In college, she found her love for reading and realized that she could have a career publishing the stories spinning in her imagination. Though she graduated with a degree in Marketing/Advertising and embarked on a stint in corporate America to pay the bills, her heart has always been with her characters. She's thrilled that she's been living her dream as a full-time author for the past nine years.

Shayla currently lives in North Texas with her wonderfully supportive husband, her daughter, and a very spoiled cat. In her "free" time, she enjoys reality TV, reading, and listening to an eclectic blend of music.

VISIT HER AT SHAYLABLACK.COM!